Call Her Majesty

Call Her Majesty
Comala Remogene

Published by BooXAI
ISBN:978-965-578-469-5

Call Her Majesty

COMALA REMOGENE

From The Brilliant Mind of
Comala Remogene

Acknowledgement

It would be remiss of me to not extend my deepest gratitude to those who made this book possible.

Firstly, what is anything without God in it? This book was brought to life merely because God gave me the knowledge, wisdom, and understanding to make it happen.

Yvonne Chance, Doreen Mayers, Roy Maynard, Velma Dennis, and Merva Jackson, thank you for encouraging me to be the best that I can be.

Sasha, Yanique, Camal, Sheron, Mario, Follan, Sheaba, Shawn, Petrina, Bajon, Stacey, Devon, Kester, Donna, Jacki, Michi, Keisha Jackson, Itory, Cory, Marcie, Bet, Roxanne, Collette, Bebbo, Peter-Gaye, Deja Jaheem, Cornilla, Lolo, Roxanne, Shellyann, Sheldon, Aunty Gealie, Claudette, Victor, Kadine, Nakeisha, and Markobarr. You all are appreciated. If I missed anyone, I love you.

My design team, thank you for the final touches.

I dedicate this book to my children.
Tafari Thomas, Patrick Maynard, and Madison Maynard.
Always remember there is no perfect road to success. Just be honest about how you get there.
Life will get you down, and that's okay. It happens to the best of us. Just get up and try again. Once you overcome a challenge, remember another one is waiting for you down the road, so brace yourself.
You cannot win every race, babies.
You have to lose sometimes.
That's what makes life so beautiful.
Remember, the past shapes the future.
I love you guys with my entire being.
To my mother, Winsome, and in loving memory of my dear father, Dehon Facey.
Nuff love.

Contents

CHAPTER 1
Left Behind

Majesty runs through the alley, breathless; she looks back at a man with a knife wearing a black ski mask, chasing her as the cold whistling wind rushes across her face. The breeze gusts through her floating weave without gravity.

Running barefoot, the tiny rocks piercing the bottoms of her perfectly manicured feet, she finds a hiding spot by the corner of a wall. She bends down, hiding, panicking, trying to catch her breath as quietly as she can, her heart beating fifty miles per hour, nauseated, chills, sharp pains in her chest, and hands shaking. The footsteps of the culprit getting closer, her anxiety gets the best of her. She scans around to find something to defend herself in case he discovers her hiding place. Quietly, she turns around. He grabs her and drags her by the hair, pulls her up. She immediately stands face to face with the monster.

"I am gonna kill you," he says, forcing the knife into her stomach as hard as he can.

She jumps up, looking around the room, feeling paranoid and afraid, rubbing her eyes, trying to make sense of her surroundings. She has had the same nightmare again. This is the third night in a row. It's but a nightmare.

Eighty-eight years old, wrinkled, and grey-haired, Majesty lies in her warm bed beside her husband Arthur as he sleeps quietly. She remembers different events that happened so she can tell her adult children, Demetre, Patrick, and Madison, about the story of her childhood and their father. They are excited to hear the rest of the story as their mother gets comfortable. She is a woman of wisdom, with decades of history hidden in her memory.

She continues. "Once upon a time . . . ."

CHAPTER 2

Family

It cannot be when the root is neglected, that what springs from it will be well ordered.
-- Confucius

Twenty-year-old Winnie Stewart, pregnant with an athletic build, has caramel brown skin and beautiful black eyes. She works in a pharmacy as a pharmacist.

Her husband, twenty-two-year-old Dehon Facey, tall and handsome, sports a low haircut that accentuates his well-defined cheekbones. He knows things are hard on his pregnant wife, who works double shifts to pay their bills on her own. He works multiple dead-end jobs that never last and do not pay him enough.

He needs to work for Bob, a drug dealer in his community, selling dime bags of weed to make some quick money, easy money, to help pay their rent and maintain their basic needs.

Dehon tells himself, "I've got a baby coming. I need to get it together. Working for Bob will be temporary." He continues, "As long as I do the right thing, say the right thing around Bob, I will be straight with him even though he is a cutthroat, backstabbing individual."

The couple gives birth on June 30, 1998, to a beautiful baby girl named Comala Diana Facey. Her dad loves her so much that he calls her Majesty. The name sticks with her, and everyone calls her by that name.

Dehon sacrifices and saves all his money. He has a plan to buy a house with cash for his family. A few years later, Winnie and Dehon purchase their beautiful home in a well-maintained, manicured community. It has three bedrooms, two bathrooms, a living room, and a perfect kitchen. It is everything Winnie could dream of. She loves to cook and chill with her amazing husband. After his daughter is born and he accomplishes his long-term goal of owning a home, he retires from selling weed and moves on with his family.

Both parents teach Majesty to learn from them to be strong, confident, and intelligent.

Winnie's best friend is a seventy-five-year-old retired soldier named Miss Mary, who lives ten feet away from them. They share recipes, and on Christmas, they exchange gifts. She is Majesty's godmother.

When Majesty turns eight years old, the pharmacy hours are reduced; no overtime, only on holidays. It really affects the Facey's household. The couple agrees for Dehon to get back in the weed game temporarily until she can pick up some more shifts. They know how dangerous the game can get with the cops.

Bob hates the fact that Dehon purchased a home and has a family. He can't stand the sight of him; envy fills his gut when he sees Dehon. *How did he do it? He bought a home, and he make way little, and I still live with my mother and sister. I need to buy a house too,* he thinks. He is known to be notorious and savage for killing many people and being their community's ruler. Whatever he says goes; that's his motto. *I'm gonna kill that fool. He thinks he's better than me,* he thinks to himself.

CHAPTER 3

Sad

On February 3, 2004, Winnie tucks her daughter in bed, reads her favorite bedtime story, prays, and kisses her.

She whispers, "Goodnight, baby girl." Majesty is quickly fast asleep but is awakened by shattered glass and strange, loud voices chattering in her living room. She jumps up, frightened, rubs her eyes, gets on her tippy toes, and peeks through the crack in her bedroom door. She sees her parents kneeling and begging for their lives. A nagging feeling of fear curls in her stomach. She knows her parents are in trouble. Three men are pointing guns at their heads.

"Where's my damn money?" shouts one of the men she recognizes.

The radio plays the low rhythm of Winnie's favorite program, "Lovers' Rock." The clock ticks in slow motion; the sofas, bookshelf, center table, and television all seem to freeze in fear as if they had a gun pointed at them. The light flickers off the radio set.

Dehon pleads for his life. "Bob, I gave you all your money last night." In a fearful voice, he says, "You were drinking beers at the dominoes table." He takes two deep breaths and continues. "Remember? I gave it to you! You must have lost it." With open palms, Dehon begs, "I've worked for you five years. I never short you a penny. Please don't

5

do this, I'll work and pay you again, please let my wife go. She has nothing to do with this."

Bob isn't listening to what he is saying, pretending he doesn't remember collecting the money.

He says, "I don't remember. I don't like a thief trying to calm his rage."

Winnie is crying and begging, "Please, Bob." The other men have their guns pointed at the back of her head.

Majesty hides as sadness fills her bedroom, peeking, hoping no one sees her. Her heart is jumping through her chest. *Should I go out and help my parents? Bob, my father's friend! He's always been nice to me. He's being cruel to my mom and dad*, she thinks.

Fear sweeps her hero's face. "Daddy," she sobs quietly as fear covers her soul. Her own vulnerability gets the best of her as tears flow down her cheeks. She tries not to make a sound. Bob marches in a circle, at times pacing across the living room, waving the gun in his hand.

She hears a loud pop. Jumps from fright. Her mother screams, dragging out the word "No." Her hand covers her mouth. Majesty's eyes go cartoon-wide as her father's lifeless body hits the floor. One of the other men then shoots her mother – *bam!* – in the temple. Her mother's lifeless body falls beside her dad's dead body. The room cries in distress. The gunpowder and smoke give off a smell like fireworks. A mixture of coal, sulfur, and potassium invades every molecule in her nostrils. The whole thing took minutes, but feels like an eternity watching the horror.

Majesty creeps under the bed as quietly as she can, shaking like a leaf, her teeth clapping together. She can't believe what she is witnessing, the thought of losing both parents. The image keeps playing in her head, hoping they don't find her hiding spot.

She hears them vandalizing the house, breaking glass. Bob orders one of the men, "Burn this damn house down, so there'll be no evidence." A few more indecent words leave his mouth.

Majesty jumps out of her window. Cold air slaps her face. Brittle leaves crunch under her feet. Staring and pacing through the darkness, she wishes she had a sweater, but it's too late now. She runs to the backyard of her neighbor, Miss Mary. She panics. Everything is pitch black;

the moon has dodged behind the clouds as she watches flames engulf her once beautiful home.

The three men jump in a white car that is parked outside of her house. Their shadows reflect under the dull light of the street pole. They enter the car and drive off, screeching on the road. Majesty comes out from hiding and looks around. The discomfort in her tummy increases at seeing what is being destroyed. She begins to cry.

Reality sets in. Her parents are murdered and burning in the fire and are gone forever. Her neighbor hugs and comforts her, putting a blanket around her tiny body. "Where are your parents?" Miss Mary asks in a concerned tone.

Majesty cries, "They are burning in the fire. I smell smoke." Her voice is shaking. "I tried to find my parents. The fire got so big that I climbed through my bedroom window to escape." Miss Mary hugs her and pulls her closer. They both watch the out-of-control fire. Smoke drifting across the roof, doors, and windows. Fire coming through every opening of the house. The smoke burning their eyes and filling their lungs, so thick and overpowering they begin to suffocate and cough. The dancing flames eat at her house like a red and black monster. The roof collapses. She cries.

Neighbors are trying to put out the fire with whatever they can use. They throw water. Nothing seems to work.

Everything is happening so fast. Majesty cries out in despair. From miles away, she hears screaming sirens coming in her direction. It's not long until the road is filled with fire trucks, ambulances, and police cars. Flashing lights dance through the night; the smell of burning tires and meat invades Majesty's nose. Everything is in slow motion.

The firefighters grab hoses from the fire trucks and spray water on the burning building; another fireman puts up a ladder and uses another hose to contain the fire so it doesn't spread.

After about an hour and thirty minutes of spraying water on the conflagration, the fire is extinguished. They rush into the house, pull the burned bodies out, put them in black body bags, and zip them. Then, put them in the ambulance. "I can't believe that's my mommy and daddy," she cries, squeezing the hips of Miss Mary. "They are gone forever."

Uniformed police cordon off the house with yellow caution tape. Reporters from the local TV channel are snapping pictures. They are trying to make sense of the scene and are trying to interview as many people as possible for the morning news.

The lead detective, Constable Mills, takes Majesty in her police car and navigates the highway to the police station. Constable Mills parks in the front parking lot. They get out of the car and walk toward the building.

The sign "Waterford Police Department" is prominently displayed on the building. It's a two-story building with triple-hung windows and glass doors. It's a beautiful modern building.

The entryway conspicuously displays an intercom system on the wall by the entry door. Glass covers the front office.

Constable Mills ushers her through the front sliding door.

Constable Joey greets them at the door. "Hey, Constable Mills," says Joey. "How's it going?"

"Busy night," she replies in a melancholy tone.

Majesty's tears flow in silence as she stares at Constable Mills.

She puts her badge on the wall pad; it beeps her in, and they enter. The other officers sit at their desks, chatting and observing Majesty as they walk by.

Majesty stares at a well-shaped police officer at her desk, clenching a telephone locked between her neck and ear as she scribbles on a note pad.

She leads Majesty to a cozy room and has her sit.

Constable Mills says in the most caring voice, "Baby girl. I'm so sorry about your mom and your dad." She pauses and continues, "Are you OK?" Kneeling and holding her hands, she whispers, "I know you don't understand now, but God will bring you through."

Majesty sighs as tears roll down her eyes.

"Would you like something to drink?" asks Constable Mills.

Two policemen walk by the room, talking about the cases they are working on, not knowing who is in the room.

Majesty shakes her head. "No," she says. Tears pour from her eyes. "Can you please call my nana?"

There are no words anyone can offer her to bring her parents back.

No relief from the pain she is feeling. She can only live with her new situation and learn as it becomes her new way of life.

Constable Mills asks, "Do you know what happened? Was your mom or dad cooking when this happened?"

"My mother read me my bedtime story; I went to bed. I smelled smoke. I opened my room door. I looked for Mom and Dad, but the fire was too much. I jumped through the window and ran to my godmother's house." She pauses with tears running down her cheeks and says, "If I had seen anything else, I'd tell you."

She thinks to herself, *Bob is very dangerous. He will kill me if I ever say anything. I will never let anyone know what I saw.*

Constable Mills gives her a business card and says, "Call this number if you remember anything else."

"I will," Majesty says.

Numbness, denial, anger, and despair are some of the emotions she is feeling.

Shortly after, her grandparents arrive. Constable Joey speaks through the walkie-talkie. "Constable Mills come in. You have Mr. and Ms. Bennis here for you."

Constable Mills replies, "Over. Can you direct them to the break room?"

"Roger that," he replies.

In a few minutes, Majesty's grandparents, Septemus and Wilma Bennis, come rushing into the room and hug Majesty as tears flow down their faces. The room is overwhelmed with sadness. They embrace her. Septemus asks, "Are you OK, Majesty?"

She shakes her head and whispers, "No."

Constable Mills introduces herself and fills them in on what happened.

They are in disbelief. Wilma asks, "Are you sure they both died?"

"Yes," Constable Mills confirms. Soon after, they leave and take Majesty home.

CHAPTER 4
Living with Grandma

Majesty sits in the back of Septemus' car. The air-conditioner fills the car with a blast of 60-degree air. She carefully wraps the warm blanket her godmother gave her over her tiny body. Septemus swiftly drives on the highway. Majesty stares intently at the moving vehicles and the blazing lights passing their car. She feels defeated and sad; she wishes this were a dream. The earth seems so calm now after Dehon's and Winnie's souls are taken to heaven. Majesty squeezes her eyes tight together as tears flow down her face. The gray sky has a dirty look.

Wilma says, "Majesty, tell me what you remember about tonight."

Majesty answers in a sad tone. "I was sleeping, and I –"

"On tonight's news." The radio interrupts her, and she abruptly stops talking. A male reporter from the local news is talking.

Septemus turns up the volume. He says, "Hold on, Majesty, let's listen to what the reporters are saying about your parents."

The news reporter continues, "Tonight in Waterford, there was a fire at approximately 8:30 p.m. Taking the lives of Winnie and Dehon Facey. The police are investigating what may have caused the fire. Sadly, the couple leaves behind their eight-year-old daughter Comala Diana Facey."

Septemus quickly turns the volume down. The news report confirms that he's in denial. He digests that his daughter is no longer with them. Silence sucks the life out of the car. His expression says it all as they approach the street they live on.

The car pulls up to the driveway. Dominique opens the front door and rushes to hug her niece. She ushers her inside. Shanda and Michie are curled up on the sofa in front of the muted TV. Majesty walks into the somber living room. Her aunts stand and rush over to embrace her. They are all crying and in disbelief. Majesty tries to process the horror her night has witnessed. Everyone's trying to wrap their heads around what happened while comforting Majesty. She stares at the muted television and presses her lips together.

Silence fills the room until Shanda says, "Maybe the stove was left on by accident, or a candle fell or something, and that's what started the fire." Shanda wipes a teardrop from her face.

Dominique chimes in, "I can't believe this is happening. They all were here eating Sunday dinner with us last week." Dominique sighs to ease the tension in her neck. She continues, "Winnie and Dehon were so happy. They were always roasting everyone. Oh God, poor Winnie." Tears stream down her face. They reminisce about the fun times.

Michie joins in. "She was so happy when she met Dehon. When he proposed, she was so beautiful and happy when she was getting married. Not to mention giving birth to Majesty."

They all start bawling. Shanda keeps her gaze on Majesty. They miss Winnie and Dehon, but more importantly, they all feel sorry for their niece.

Wilma asks, "Majesty, you were sleeping? Finish telling me what happened."

She shivers under their tight gaze. "I was sleeping." Majesty's words grab everyone's attention. She continues, "I smelled smoke, so I opened my room door. The fire was so big, and the heat was hot. I jumped through my window and ran to Miss Mary's backyard."

More pain announces itself. She sobs. They comfort Majesty, reassuring her she will be OK.

Wilma glances at the clock on the wall. It's 11:45 p.m. She says, "It's time for bed." She leads Majesty to her mother's bedroom. She says, "This is where you will be staying."

Majesty's eyes search the room. Winnie's stuff is still in the same place where she left it. The bed, nightstand, and dresser are so organized, and her flowery, soft pink comforter is neatly spread on her bed. Makeup, hairspray, and perfume are placed on the dresser. A picture of her younger self in her school uniform rests in a picture frame on the wall. *Tick-tock* sounds the alarm clock sitting on the nightstand.

She walks over to the bed and rubs her hand over the soft comforter, then lies down and swallows. Drawing in a long breath to calm her anxiety. Tears stream down her face. Wilma asks, "Do you want me to stay with you tonight?"

Majesty lowers her voice to a whisper. "No, I am fine."

Wilma gives her a T-shirt; she hugs her and kisses her on the forehead. She says, "Good night, Majesty, everything is going to be OK." She leaves the door ajar.

Majesty lies in her mother's bed, and she prays. "Lord, please help me. I miss Mommy and Daddy."

Sleeping in her mother's childhood bed is hard for her. She can't sleep. The nightmares seem so real and are overtaking her anxiety. She envisions the monster Bob and his friends chasing her to kill her. Her heart hammers in her chest. She jumps out of her sleep. Majesty spends a significant portion of her time in bed awake. The ordeal replays in her mind.

Wilma gives her a bag of new clothes, underwear, shoes, and slippers the following morning. Majesty places the contents on the bed and scans them. She has everything she needs. Her family will take the best care of her. Her aunts are so excited to have her. To them, she is their human doll. They will take turns washing and combing her hair. They love her.

Her grandparents have a plan. They will give Majesty love and care. They will provide security and a sense of belonging, with open communication making her feel safe, important, and valued.

In thirty minutes, she showers, dresses, slips her bare feet into her slippers, and heads to the living room, the smell of bacon and eggs filling the house. As she walks into the kitchen, Wilma is cooking up a storm.

"Hi, Grandma," she says. Hyperventilating, she quietly tries slowing down her breathing.

Two pots and a frying pan sit on the stovetop. On the clean counter rests a basket of bread. Magnet fruits are stuck on the refrigerator door. She pours some orange juice into one of the cups. Wilma is excited to see her grandbaby. "Hi, Majesty. Did you sleep well? Please sit at the table. I cooked some eggs and bacon for you."

Majesty whispers, "OK." She sips her orange juice, places it on the table, and then sits. Wilma swiftly walks over to where Majesty sits. She lays the plate of eggs, bacon, and toast in front of her. Majesty picks at the meal for thirty minutes. She isn't hungry. Her thoughts are fixated on how much she misses her parents. Wilma's attention locks on Majesty. She notices Majesty's expression is blank. She hasn't touched her meal.

Wilma arches her eyebrow. She says, "Baby when you're finished eating, you can cover the leftovers for later."

She says, "Thank you." Majesty shifts away from the table. Wilma's gaze meets hers. Majesty walks over to the kitchen; there are two plates deposited in the sink. She covers what is left of her meal and returns to her bedroom.

Majesty lacks interest in fun activities, has no appetite, and is constantly plagued by nightmares. She feels sad, hopeless, and has low energy. The family is so concerned. They miss Winnie and Dehon. They have to help Majesty through this difficult time. They listen to her attentively and affirm her feelings. Wilma shares other people's experiences and lets her know her parents are watching over her.

They teach her everything. They want her to be very independent; she has a set of chores. One Saturday, Wilma says, "Majesty, even though your parents are not here with us, I want you to be able to help yourself." She teaches her how to use the washing machine and how to clean her bedroom.

* * *

After two weeks, an appointment is set with Constable Mills. Dehon's parents, Merkle and Kester Facey, arrive at the Bennises' house. Kester says, "Good to see you, Septemus."

Septemus replies, "Good to see everyone. How are you holding up? How is my grand baby?" He lets them in the house.

Kester holds his arms outstretched, waiting for his hug and kisses from his granddaughter. Majesty glides over to her grandfather's hug and kisses him. And then she hugs and kisses Merkle. Merkle squeezes her an extra three seconds as she embraces her.

They greet everyone. They all gather in the living room. Septemus makes room at the other end of the dining table for Merkle and Kester. Two jugs are placed on the table; the contents have water and juice to accommodate the guests. The muted TV set is playing a commercial. Majesty sits with her nana, Wilma. Dominique, Shanda, and Michie cuddle up on the sofa making suggestions about the funeral arrangements. Michie says, "Winnie loved white. I think we should have them in gold and white caskets."

Dominique chimes in, "I think that's a great idea."

Wilma asks, "How are you, Mrs. Merkle?"

Mrs. Merkle shakes her head vigorously and replies, "We are not doing too bad."

Suddenly, the doorbell rings, and the conversations freeze.

Shanda gets up and glides to the front door. "Good afternoon, Constable Mills. You can come in; we are expecting you."

Constable Mills says, "Hello. Good afternoon." She enters and introduces herself. "Thank you for welcoming me to your home. Condolences. How is Majesty? How is she adjusting to her new environment?" She looks at Majesty and says, "How are you, Majesty?" Everyone drags their stares from the police to Majesty.

Majesty answers, "I am fine." She wears a stretched smile.

Shanda points to the empty sofa that is awaiting her presence. She says, "Have a seat. Shanda asks, "Can I get you anything to drink, Constable Mills?"

She replies, "No, thank you. I am sorry for your loss. I came here to let you know what came up on the autopsy." She walks over to the sofa with a folder she holds in her hand and sits. It gets so quiet if a pin drops you can hear it. She opens the folder, takes a deep breath, and begins. "Dehon and Winnie were shot in their heads, execution style, with two different firearms. That discharged different bullet rounds. There's more than one person of interest."

Kester buries his chin in the palm of his hand.

She continues, "Before the killers fled, they burned the house down to make it look like a fire accident. The case is now a homicide." Everyone studies Constable Mills' expression. Merkle closes her eyes and shakes her head. The family starts crying all over again.

Adrenaline surges up Majesty's spine. *Can I please wake up, Lord, from this horrible dream? I want to go home.* Her bright gaze stares at her family. She continues thinking. *I want my mommy and daddy.* She already knew all that; she saw it unfold right before her eyes. It's hard to hear the police lady talking about what she already knows.

Everyone is heartbroken; they all thought the stove was left on. Maybe a candle, a match, and an accident happened. They didn't know someone was out there alive who murdered their loved ones. They all are in disbelief.

"It is crystal-clear that this is a murder," Merkle sobs with her hands on her head and her chin slouched on her chest. Her high-pitched cries fill the living room.

The melancholy feeling floats and suffocates the room. Constable Mills asks, with a notepad taking notes, "Would anyone want to kill either of them?" Everyone is clueless.

Wilma answers. "They were good kids. High school sweethearts. They worked so hard and bought their first home. They loved everybody, and everyone loved them." She wails, "How could a mother bury her child?"

Wilma chimes in, "Lord, please take this case. Whoever killed our family, bring them to justice." She bursts out in a loud cry. Tiny streams of liquid roll down her face. Septemus tries to hold back tears, trying to comfort his wife.

CHAPTER 5

The Funeral

On February 10, 2 p.m., friends and family fill the church for Winnie and Dehon's funeral. Everyone wears black or dark clothes. Dehon and Winnie are lying in matching white and gold caskets. A projector displays photos of the couple one picture at a time. When younger Winnie had her missing tooth. In her school uniform. Winnie and Dehon's first date. Dehon as a teenager. Dehon and his mother, Merkle. The couple getting married. Winnie showing her baby bump. Graduating in her gown. The birth of Majesty. Multiple pictures of them and Majesty as a family. Two large still pictures of Winnie and Dehon are placed front and center beside both caskets. Flowers are everywhere; it's like a garden. The pianist sits and plays mournful songs.

The ushers distribute programs with the itinerary of the service to everyone when entering the church.

The front row seats the family. Majesty sits between Michie and Dominique. Majesty crosses her legs, looking pointedly at her parents' pictures. Wilma, Septemus, Merkle, Kester, Shanda, and Miss Mary all sit together. Sadness fills the oxygen in the church. The mourners are whispering.

Dominique whispers, "Are you OK, Majesty?" Shaking her head from left to right,

Majesty says, "I miss them." Tears roll down her face. She continues, "Why can't I see my parents for the last time?"

Michie joins in; her whispering voice cracks. "Baby, your parents were badly burned. You wouldn't recognize them if they open the casket." Michie, fanning herself with the program, continues. "They want us to have great memories, so they keep the caskets closed."

The pastor walks to the podium and stares across the entire church. Holding the mike, he begins with a prayer. After he finishes praying, he begins to preach. "Who would want to murder these beautiful souls? Their lives were cut short." He continues to ask questions everyone wants to know. "Who kill my beloved brother Dehon and his beautiful wife, Winnie? I preached at their wedding." He marches from left to right of the podium. Staring at the audience, he continues. "They were so excited to join hands in matrimony." He trades a glance with Majesty and points at her. "I baptized their amazing daughter Majesty." He continues, "Majesty, just know we love you. Winnie and Dehon were so beautiful God wanted them in heaven. God took them to heaven to be angels, to watch over us. Let us honor the life of Mr. Dehon and Winnie Facey."

The pianist plays "When the Roll Is Called Up Yonder, I'll Be There." Everyone sings along.

Family members who are listed in the program go to the podium one by one to speak about the memories of Winnie and Dehon. Michie sings a tune. Shanda approaches the podium. As she steers at the audience, she gives a stretched smile and adjusts the microphone. "Hello everyone." She reads a chapter from the bible. Majesty sits and stares at the large picture of them as she brushes the tears from her face. Miss Mary reads the eulogy. She works through crying to get out what needs to be said.

When it is Septemus's turn, he says, "Thank you for helping us through this trying time. We had no idea where to begin. Each of you plays an important role. The outpouring of support. We appreciate the compassion you all show our family at this difficult time. Death is tough. This is affecting our family." The balled-up tissue he has in his hand he uses to wipe his tears. He continues, "Please continue praying for our family. Life is so short. Let's live the rest of our lives with great memories." He picks up the paper that he carries with him and leaves the podium. Dominique rubs Majesty's back, comforting her. She holds her tiny hands in hers. The funeral is sweet sorrow. The moments of raw pain. The service screams in silent anguish.

After the service, the funeral home staff leads everyone in a straight line. Six pallbearers carry Winnie's casket, following the six pallbearers carrying Dehon's casket. Majesty marches behind, reminiscing on all the fun times she had with her parents. She scans through the crowd. She spots Bob and his friends. She is startled. Interrupting her thoughts, she straightens her dress. She tries to hold her composure, then takes a deep breath. Her heart is racing. She clenches her teeth and cringes hard.

Miss Mary walks over to where Majesty is standing. Every wrinkle on her face shows every birthday. She pulls Majesty aside and says, "Majesty, your parents loved you very much. Winnie was my best friend. I am your godmother. Whatever you need, don't hesitate to ask me."

Majesty replies, "Thank you." Miss Mary hugs and squeezes her so tight.

The pallbearers take her parents to their final resting place. She marches behind the caskets. Everyone walks briskly. It is very somber. The family and friends can't contain themselves. They are all crying and mourning; it is so emotional, not to mention Kester and Merkle can't control themselves. It is a very sad situation.

Bob walks over to her and says in a concerned tone. "Majesty, I am so sorry for your loss. Did you see the killers?" He anxiously awaits her response.

She shakes her head and says, "No."

He replies in a soft tone, "A police officer came to our neighborhood asking questions. Her name is Constable Mills. She told us someone shot both your parents in the head and set the house on fire. Just keep being strong. If you hear anything, let me know. Your father was my best friend. He was a good man, and your mother, too." He glances at Miss Mary and continues, "It's a shame how they killed them. Let me know if you need anything."

Majesty shakes her head. She scrutinizes Bob and his friends as they are pretending they care. She can't believe how dangerous these men are. The mischievous laugh and guilt in his eyes. Tears fill her eyes. She feels helpless. She says, "OK." He walks away. She mutters to herself, "Killers, I will get you, just wait." She makes a promise as she watches the funeral director slowly lower her parent's caskets. They treat the process with respect, care, and empathy. She says to herself, "I am going to kill all of them."

CHAPTER 6

Transition

Wilma and Septemus take Majesty to church with them every Sunday. Majesty hates going there; she would rather stay home and watch cartoons. Whenever she's in the sanctuary, she feels a connection with God. She remembers her mom praying for her the night of their murder. The feeling she senses, she knows that she belongs in the presence of the Lord. It is unexplainable. She tries not to think about it too much.

Majesty has become friends with her neighbor Antwan. He is her best friend. They play a lot of dollhouse games and hide and seek. He becomes her boyfriend. They share stories and have a few things in common. Antwan stays with his aunt and cousin. His parents live in Canada. He breaks her virginity on her 12th birthday. He is kind, loving, and the sweetest person. They hang out all the time, and she loves his company. He teaches her everything she knows. She is in love with him. Whenever she's around him, she doesn't think about her parents; he fills the gap. A few years later, Antwan migrates to Canada. Once again, little Majesty is left behind. She says to herself, "Anyone I love always leaves."

School is becoming very difficult for Majesty. A bully called Kendon Gardon always picks on her. She is so scared of him. He always takes away her lunch money, and when she refuses, he gives her a beating. She doesn't tell anyone she is being bullied.

On Saturdays, Septemus loves watching boxing. Majesty makes it her priority to tune in with him. Learning new moves. She is getting ready to beat the hell out of Bob. The more she watches the fighters, the more confident she feels through a fist.

She says to herself, "I will not let that boy take my money anymore." The next day, she is ready to put a stop to it. When she sees him, a lump grows in her throat. She ends up choking. She gets scared and hands him the money. Majesty is so afraid of Kendon Gardon that she feels powerless whenever she sees him.

She should be thinking about learning, but she is thinking about how hungry she is after giving up her lunch money. She misses her parents. She must stop this bully once and for all from taking her lunch money. He has done that for a while.

Monday afternoon, he comes to her and says, "Yow, where's my money?" She is so fed up with him, she doesn't answer him. He punches her in the face.

Majesty looks at him with rage. After watching boxing, she has the confidence she needs. She gives him an ass whipping. She punches him repeatedly. All her emotions, pain, and sadness get the best of her. Her losing her parents. She can't control herself. Punching on repeat with all her might. She doesn't feel that her skin is torn. She is numb. Blood flowing from her hands. She's in another dimension. Majesty imagines punching and beating Bob's face. The students stop cheering. They become so quiet. They are scared and worried for Kendon. Miss Mattis and Mr. Panton, the principal, run over to them. They drag her off him.

Mr. Panton and Miss Mattis lead them to his office. He opens the door. And orders Majesty, "Sit in the chair over there." She sits nonchalantly. She snatches a glance in Kendon's direction. She has a smirk on her face. Kendon's face looks as if he went through a tornado. Blood is dripping like a pipe. Miss Mattis gives her a napkin for her hands to stop the bleeding. The principal directs Kendon across the hallway to the sick bay. The school nurse rushes to his aid.

Within an hour, Wilma comes busting through the door. She sees Majesty, and her heart drops. She gives her a reassuring look. She heads to the principal. He leads them to take the first right and enter a quiet room. Miss Mattis is already seated, with three chairs and a table. She gestures for them to sit.

He says, "I am sorry to have you rushing over here, Ms. Bennis." Wilma looks at her. "Comala was in a fight. This is out of her character. Comala is an honor roll student very quiet. I have never had a complaint about your granddaughter. Since she lost her parents, she has become very distant."

Miss Mattis asks, "Comala, do you want to tell us what started the fight?" They all gaze at her.

Majesty replies in a soft tone, "Kendon is always bullying and threatening me. He takes away my lunch money every day. If I refuse to give it to him like today, he fights me. I never want any trouble, so I hand my money to him. I just couldn't take it anymore. Because I stood up to him this time, that's what happened."

Wilma chimes in, "This boy is out of line. My grandbaby is going through a lot right now. He is putting pressure on her. I thought this was a safe place for her." Tears run down her face.

Mr. Panton joins in. "This young man is a troublemaker. Every day, I get a complaint from his teacher. He is always bullying students. I need an intervention with his parents. I will have Comala return tomorrow for school. Do you have any questions for me?"

Wilma says, "No." They say their goodbyes.

Majesty goes back to her class and gathers her belongings. The students are happy. Majesty is not the only one he's been bullying. From that day on, she realizes bullying is just intimidation and mind over matter. She gets respect from her peers.

They exit the school compound. They walk to the parking lot. The temperature increases to an uncomfortable level. Majesty's idle feet drag her. If she walks any further, she will look like she just got out of a sauna. She is bobbing up and down towards the parked car. When she sits in the passenger seat, Wilma says, "Baby, why didn't you tell me this was happening? I feel like I failed you, honey."

Majesty replies, "No, Grandma, you didn't fail me."

"You are going through a lot."

"I didn't want to be a burden."

Merkle says, "Don't you ever think you are causing a problem, or being a burden. Please tell me when something is not going right. I am so proud of you for defending yourself. I am your granny. I will never be your mother. I will always catch you if you fall. I love you." She holds her hands. "Remember, obstacles will come. It is how you finish your race. It is not how you start it. Power is about strength. Never give the enemy an opening." She hugs and kisses her. She glimpses at her busted hands. "You got this, Majesty." They both laugh.

Majesty attends the best high school in the country. She is focused on her education. She maintains honor roll status. Majesty is always at the top of her class. The loss of her parents doesn't stop her from excelling. She gets awards and certificates. Wilma is so proud of her. She knows she is destined to be great someday. She thinks to herself that she wishes her parents could be here to see how well she is turning out.

* * *

The grandparents on both sides file a claim with the insurance company on behalf of Majesty. She is the beneficiary after the passing of her parents. The claims are approved. Wilma and Merkle hire a contractor and a subcontractor. They rebuild the house for Majesty. They will give her the keys on her 18th birthday. In the meantime, they will rent it out and save the money for her to attend college.

Merkle knows Majesty is having a hard time. A change of scenery would give her a different outlook on life. She takes her to the American embassy and gets her an American Visa. Merkle and Wilma plan a three-day vacation for the summer.

Wilma says, "I think taking her to Miami with you is a great idea. This trip can take things off of her mind."

Merkle replies, "I hope so. I lost my son. It's so hard for me. I miss him so much. I cannot sleep at night. I can't stop thinking about the torture they endured before they killed them." She shakes her head. "Majesty lost both of her parents. I can imagine what she is going through."

Wilma chimes in, "I keep remembering Winnie. I really miss her. She was such a sweetheart."

Majesty is so excited to go on a plane. The night of the trip, she sleeps by Merkle's house. They arrive at the airport on time. Majesty holds her pink suitcase and stands with her grandma in the airport. They go through a long line to check-in. They stroll through the aisle with their luggage. Merkle spots the seat numbers. She takes both suitcases and puts them in the overhead compartment. Majesty slides over to the window seat. Merkle sits beside her. Before takeoff, a beautiful, uniformed flight attendant not older than 25 stands in the aisle and speaks through an intercom.

She says, "Good afternoon, ladies and gentlemen. Please be seated and fasten your seat belt. At this time, secure all baggage underneath your seat or in the overhead compartments. We also ask that your seats and table trays are in the upright position for takeoff."

Suddenly, the plane takes off. It's nerve-wracking for Majesty. She grabs the seat tight. Gravity pulls her head to the back of the chair. She squeezes her eyes tight and panics as the aircraft climbs quickly. Once airborne, it glides and cruises. Majesty relaxes, feeling like she is in a moving car. The ride becomes bumpy again. Merkle sees the fear in her eyes. She reassures her the plane is going through the clouds. "Is called turbulence," she says,

Everything seems calm. Majesty looks through the window. She admires and imagines the shaping of each cloud. Her mind jogs to her parents. Wishing she is going to see them. Shortly, the trip comes to an end.

They deplane. They join the line to go through immigration. When it is their turn, the officer flips the pages of their passports. He takes their pictures. He takes their fingerprints. He grants them six months in the country.

Majesty stares at the travelers. Families of every race and culture rush through the airport. The passengers are trying to catch their flights, speeding through terminals and heading to baggage claim. *This place is so busy*, she thinks.

They go outside and hop in a taxi. They drive on the busy highway. Merkle notices Majesty admiring the view from the back seat window. She smiles. The traffic jams on the street, motorbikes, and trucks traveling in different directions. The taxi driver takes them to The Grand

Buff Road Hotel. He unloads their baggage. Majesty steps out and takes in how beautiful the building is. Merkle pays the driver.

They enter the beautiful hotel lobby, check in at the front desk, and go to their room.

It is 900 square feet, with 12-foot ceilings. It has two beds and one bathroom. The view showcases the perfect hotel pool. The television is placed on the wall. A table and two side tables decorate the room, along with a mini fridge and ironing board.

Merkle tosses the keys on the table. They place the suitcases beside the beds. Majesty stares through the window, watching the guest swimming in the hotel pool. *This is so much fun,* she thinks.

Majesty takes a shower. They order room service, and she tunes in to the Disney Channel.

The following morning, they go to the shopping district in downtown Miami. There are lots of boutiques, art to bargain for, and high-end items. The inconsistent weather is unpredictable in Florida. One minute, it's pouring rain. The next minute, it's sunny. They walk with an umbrella at all times.

Merkle buys her underwear, shoes, clothes, and toys. After shopping and a long day, the taxi drives them back to the hotel. *This is the best trip ever,* she thinks. Later that night, they have dinner at an upscale restaurant. They are seated by the waitress. Majesty straightens the tablecloth soon after, and the server places shrimp scampi in front of Merkle and chicken and fried rice in front of Majesty.

Merkle prays for the food. They both say amen. Merkle spreads out her napkin. She says, "Majesty, I know you are going through a rough time. Just trust the process. Those people who killed your parents years ago still didn't get arrested. It's going to be OK. Time will solve the case. God will take care of those murderers."

She picks up her fork with pasta on it and puts it in her mouth. She looks at Majesty. Majesty bites her chicken. Then nods and replies, "I know Grandma."

Merkle says, "I never expected to lose my son so young. I thought he would die old. He was such a caring person. He loved you so much." She looks distant as she nods.

Majesty feels the grief increase again. She bites her chicken. She picks up a fork full of rice and shoves it in her mouth. Merkle sips her drink and presses her lips together, and she lifts her fork again. After dinner, the waitress clears the table and hands them the check.

They head to the hotel room and watch her favorite movie. The next morning, they go sightseeing. She has a lot of fun. Merkle is so happy to see Majesty pulled out of her funk.

A few days later, they arrive at Montego Bay International Airport. The trip was a great experience. It was short but so much fun. It cleared her mind and took it off her sadness.

CHAPTER 7

Red Rose

Wilma sees Miss Mary at the market one Saturday. They are so excited to see each other, catching up on Majesty's growth and how she is getting ready for college. Miss Mary asks, "How is my goddaughter? Can she visit and spend one weekend with me?"

Wilma knows she is Winnie's best friend. The last time she saw her was at her funeral. She replies, "I will talk to her. She will let me know if she wants to come by." They exchange phone numbers. "I will call you and let you speak with her."

Two weeks later, Wilma and Majesty drive into Waterford. They pass through a winding road. Houses are packed beside each other on the curbs. A large streetlight pole stands at attention. Landmarks are visible, as well as shops. A lady rides a bicycle along the road beside Wilma's car. Majesty hasn't been in Waterford since her parent's murder. This place still has a hold on her. It's such a neat place, and she misses it there. Wilma pulls into her parent's street and Miss Mary's driveway.

She takes a deep breath. And a long gaze at her parent's once-happy house. It's newly built and beautiful. Every fiber of hair stands at attention. As she stares, Majesty quickly thinks about her mom and dad.

That is now a blur in her memory. Living there are the last memories of them. She misses it. She is happy her grandparents didn't sell the property. They kept it for when she turned 18 years of age. She had been sad for a long time, but she is in a better place now. Being there brings back so many memories. Her grandparents have it rented to a nice couple.

She kisses Wilma, says goodbye, and takes her backpack out. She walks toward the door, rings the bell, and waits. Looking back over her shoulder, she watches Wilma drive off. The door pushes open, and Miss Mary appears.

"Hello, beautiful Majesty. How are you?" She gives her a big hug and squeezes her tight. "How old are you now, young lady?"

Miss Mary steps back, observing Majesty. Up and down, admiring how big she has gotten. She stands with her hand on her hip. Majesty smiles. She fishes her hands in her pockets, rocks from side to side, and grins. "It's good to see you too. I am OK. I am seventeen years old."

Miss Mary replies, "Your grandma told me you are on the honor roll and heading to college. You are so smart. I am so proud of you."

Miss Mary propels her inside the living room. Majesty's eye focuses on the shotgun that hangs on the wall, along with pictures of Miss Mary's younger self in her soldier's uniform, holding big guns. A sofa, center table, cabinet, TV stand, and dining table are neatly displayed.

She leads her to a bedroom. She says, "This is where you will be staying whenever you visit. You can settle in. I will get dinner ready." She disappears and heads to the kitchen.

Majesty says, "OK." She puts her bag back down. She takes off her shoes, sits in the chair, and crosses her legs.

Within an hour, Miss Mary calls her for dinner. The house is filled with a delicious aroma.

They sit at the table. The meal is prepared and neatly served. She prays for the food. They begin to eat. Mary says, "Your mother was so much fun. She was the life of the party. She was so happy when you were born. I miss her so much. I wanted you to visit me." Her voice is calm and direct. "I want to teach you how to defend yourself. What happened to your parents that night will never happen to you. I worked in the army for years. Now retired. Before you leave here, you will learn how to fire a gun and use a knife." She stares into her eyes. "Winnie was my best friend. I miss her every day. Dehon loved her so much. They were always goofing around with each other. She would be so proud of you. You look just like her. I will help you to catch those killers." Miss Mary's eyes watch for her reaction. "Did you see anything that night?"

For the first time, she feels it is OK to tell what happened that night. She feels so comfortable in Miss Mary's presence.

Majesty's eyes travel over Miss Mary's profile; her eyes, nose, and neck tell years of wisdom. Majesty says softly, "That night, my mother tucked me in bed. I fell asleep. I heard shouting, so I peeked through the door crack." Her voice begins to shiver. She continues. "I saw my father's friend Bob and two of his friends. They had guns. Bob was asking for his money." Tears stream down her face as she remembers the ordeal. "My father was explaining he paid him. Daddy said to Bob, 'You were drinking at the dominoes table when I gave you the money. I'm willing to work and pay you again.' He shot my father in the head, and the other guy shot my mother in her temple. Bob told them to burn down the house. I jumped through the window and hid in your backyard." She continues, "Bob and his followers attended my parent's funeral. He asked me if I saw anything and if I knew who killed them, I should let him know. I said, 'No, I never saw anything.'"

After Majesty tells her the details and why she didn't tell anyone, Miss Mary shakes her head. She says, "OK, do you know where they live?"

Majesty replies, "Yes, Bob lives in my grandmother Merkle's community. I see him all the time. He lives with his elder mother and his sister."

Miss Mary replies, "Good. So, we hunt them when you turn 18 on your parent's memorial. That's when we strike. I will get you prepared. I want you to catch those killers and have no mercy on those lowlifes. Majesty, are you with me?"

Majesty replies, "I want to kill him for the pain and suffering they caused my family. I just didn't know how to do it."

Majesty is excited to hear Miss Mary's plans. She wants to kill Bob. She has no clue how to get it done. *This is the perfect opportunity. I didn't know she was in the army. That explains that big gun on her wall.*

Her as a young woman holding those big rifles in those pictures, thinks Majesty.

Majesty says, "I appreciate your help," rolling her eyes and sighing. She is relieved to get training. Her cheeks are flushed. The conversation is intriguing. She stares at her barely-touched food.

Miss Mary says, "Go ahead, eat." The room becomes completely quiet. The clock ticks away. She says, "Take a shower. Go to bed; tomorrow is a long day."

The following morning, Miss Mary takes her to the mountains. The breath of fresh air overpowers Majesty's nostrils. She loves the scent of the natural crisp air. Miss Mary spreads all the guns, a silencer, and a bulletproof vest on a sheet on the car bonnet. Miss Mary teaches her everything about each weapon and how they work. She shows her what each of them can do.

They trod through the woods. Miss Mary hands her a 45 mm pistol. She places seven bottles on a rock and tells Majesty to hit as many as she can. Majesty misses every one of them. Miss Mary teaches her how to aim at her targets. She explains the difference between the high-powered weapons. Miss Mary says in a stern voice, "Majesty there is no going back. Once you kill Bob, you are a completely different person. You will develop coldness in your heart for suckers like him."

Majesty practices shooting hundreds of rounds. She ignores the hurt of her fingers. "If this is what it takes to kill Bob." She fires another shot, aiming at her target. *I have to get it done,* she thinks.

Miss Mary says, "You're doing great. You have to be careful. You cannot let anyone know what we will be doing on the weekends. That scumbag Bob should not be breathing. He is pure evil, and he had the audacity to attend your parent's funeral."

They practice every weekend. The following week, she notices a punching bag in one of Miss Mary's rooms. Miss Mary tells her, "Punch it with all your might. This is what we are practicing this weekend."

She releases all the pain on the bag. Her hand is sore when she finishes that weekend.

Miss Mary teaches her to drive. The following week, Miss Mary has her drive them to the gun range. Majesty continues practicing. She learns to reload the gun clips in a few seconds. She does a lot of push-ups and exercises. What was hard becomes so easy for her. She loves the exercise regimens.

On many occasions, they drive by Bob's house, mapping out the area. One evening, Bob is chilling, playing dominoes with a group of men. Majesty gives him a death stare in Miss Mary's tinted car. They drive past him that night.

Miss Mary says, "You will get the opportunity. Just keep practicing. There is no room for mistakes. Get your ducks in a row." Majesty understands it will take time to plan.

On her 18th birthday, Wilma hands her the keys to her parent's house. It is beautiful and furnished with brand-new furniture. Her grandparents and aunts accompanied her. When she walks in for the first time, her heart skips a beat. She visualizes the wicked ordeal that happened. Her supportive family stays with her until 10 o'clock that night, until she is settled down in her new nest. Wilma and Merkle are so overprotective.

"Are you sure you are OK being here all alone?" asks Merkle in a concerned tone.

She replies, "I am fine. Miss Mary is right next door if I need anything." They all kiss her and tell her goodbye.

Michie says, "Call me if you need company." They laugh, and they drive off.

Miss Mary comes over shortly after they leave. She hands her a box with a pistol, a silencer, and a set of bullets. She says, "You keep this close to you in this house."

She really loves Miss Mary. She is like a mother to her. She understands why she was her mom's best friend. Miss Mary's house becomes her safe place. She is there every weekend, practicing and perfecting her craft.

Majesty hangs pictures of her parents and her on the walls. She misses her mom and dad. She says in a convincing tone, in the same spot where they murdered her parents, "I am coming for you, Bob."

She continues to work out. She loves to jog, builds her muscles, and visualizes killing Bob and his followers every day. "I cannot wait to see him beg for mercy." Getting revenge gives her a reason to live every day. *Just get stronger. Just be patient*, she thinks while jogging one afternoon.

Majesty gets a part-time job as a secretary. She attends college. Majesty purchases a black Honda Accord. Every evening, she walks to Miss Mary's for her dinner, and they go over the planning and preparation.

She has less than seven months until the big day. She can't wait for Miss Mary to say, "Let's go."

At home, she cooks, cleans, attends work and school, and, most importantly, trains. Her schedule is very hectic. Miss Mary gives her a black military outfit and a ski mask. She is ready, fit, strong. She has no fear. No remorse about killing Bob and his friends.

On February 3, the night of her parents' memorial, she dresses in her all-black military outfit, bulletproof vest, balaclava, a loaded gun with a silencer tucked in her waist, and a second gun attached to her ankle holster. She slides on her brass-knuckled gloves. She packs rope, duct tape, a bottle of gasoline, a lighter, a knife, and a red rose in a small bag and places it on her back.

She says, "I am ready to do this. I have been waiting so long for this night to come."

Miss Mary replies, "Majesty, look at me." Majesty looks into her eyes. She continues, "There is no room for error. You practiced this over and over. Bob is very dangerous. If you give him an opportunity, he will kill you. Be careful. You got this."

They drive through the winding road in the dark. The passing streetlights swiftly flash behind the car. The road is quiet. A few vehicles pass by. Miss Mary drives past Bob, laughing and having fun at the dominoes table. She takes Majesty to the drop-off point. She gives her an approving look and then drives off.

Majesty enters from the back street. She has practiced this route many times. She shuffles through the road quietly in her full black outfit that blends in with the dark. She climbs Bob's neighbor's housetop and sneaks into Bob's backyard. She peeks through his window, staring intently into his house. She knows he is at the dominoes table. He is getting drunk at this hour. She thinks to herself, *Bob must die tonight.*

She needs to get inside before he gets home. She uses a bobby pin to unlock the back door. She quietly opens the door and closes it behind her. The sink of dirty dishes smells a few days old. The dripping pipe beats on a plate. The pungent scent of the trash can invades her nostrils.

She takes out her gun. Quietly, she looks into the first room. She sees his elderly, sick mother sleeping in her bed. She moves across the hall. His adult sister is watching TV. Majesty quietly scans the whole house. No one else is there. She goes back and points the gun at his sister.

Majesty commands, "Don't move." His sister jumps from fright. Majesty summons her to sit on a chair in the living room. Pulling out the rope, she commands, "If you scream, I'll kill you." She ties her up with a piece of the rope and puts duct tape on her mouth. Majesty goes into his mother's bedroom. She ties her hands to the bedhead and her legs to the footpost. She places duct tape on her mouth. Tears run down his mother's face. She gathers another chair and turns off all the lights. She is waiting patiently for Bob. She doesn't say a word. She just sits and watches them crying. She fishes in her pocket, grabs her phone, and dials Miss Mary's phone number.

The vibrating of the phone makes Miss Mary jump. Miss Mary is anticipating the call. She answers, "Hello."

Majesty replies, "Step one is complete." Majesty ends the call and places the phone back in her pocket. The mother and the sister are bawling quietly. Majesty has no remorse; she doesn't care. She is just getting started, waiting for her target.

A few moments later, Bob and three of his friends arrive at his doorway. They are laughing and staggering drunk. They are making fun of each other. Majesty stands inside, by the front doorway. When they enter, she shoots the three men in their heads. *Pow-pow-pow.* Their lifeless bodies drop to the ground.

She points the gun at Bob and orders him to sit down. He is so terrified. She ties him up and turns on the light. He sees his sister tied to the chair.

He says, "What did I do to you?" Looking around at his lifeless friends and staring at his sister, he continues, "Who are you?"

She walks over to his sister and shoots her in the temple. The bullet lodges in her head. Blood splashes on the wall and furniture. Her lifeless body hangs over the chair. Majesty looks into his eyes. She says, "Eye for an eye."

He weeps. "Please stop. What did I do to you? Please don't hurt me. I have money in the room," he says fearfully. She takes off her mask and reveals her identity. His Adam's apple jumps. His eyes bulge out. He says, "Majesty, what are you doing?" She stares dead into his eyes.

She replies, "You murdered my parents and burned my house down. I saw you."

He quickly remembers what he did to her parents.

She punches him in the face with all her might. She tases him repeatedly. She walks over to his crying mother's room. She shoots her in her temple. She sees fear in his eyes. She says, "Tooth for a tooth." Blood leaks like a pipe from his mother's head.

He wails. He knows, at this point, he is in trouble. A shining light slivers through the blinds. A vehicle passes through the empty road. He swiftly glimpses into the light. Hoping help is coming to his rescue. The vehicle speeds past his house.

He knows this is the end for him. She punches him in the face repeatedly with the brass knuckle gloves. All the years of suffering. What her family endured. She can't stop beating his face. Blood is dripping. She tases him repeatedly. She shoots him in both legs. In his spine.

He begs in a weak voice, "Please, Majesty, I beg you. I am sorry. Please stop."

She watches him suffer. It gives her the gratification she craves, satisfying her ego. She finally gets closure. She says, "This is your payback. Confess my father gave you your money."

He says in a painful voice, "Please forgive me. Your father was a good man. Dehon did pay me." He stares in wide-eyed silence, in excruciating pain. He continues, "I was jealous of him. I killed your parents."

She has no more use for his weak, frail body. She wraps her fingers tightly around her gun. She finished what is left in the clip in his head. Execution style. Blood splatters across the sofa. She sprays gasoline all over the dead bodies. She sets the place on fire. The flames become bigger. She throws the red rose on Bob and says, "I love you, Mommy and Daddy."

She exits through the back door. She disappears into thin air. Miss Mary is waiting at the pickup point on the empty road. She jumps in the car and says, "It's done." They watch from a distance as the house engulfs in flames. His neighbors rush in, trying to put the fire out.

When she gets home, Miss Mary asks. "Do you want me to stay with you tonight?"

She replies, "No. I am fine." She enters her parents' house. Miss Mary and Majesty never speak about that night ever again.

A few weeks later, Majesty attends Bob's funeral. She wears a black dress, a big black hat that covers half her face, dark glasses, and bright red lipstick, along with a red rose matching her lipstick. She enters the funeral service. She takes one of the programs. She sits and listens to the mournful messages. She strides with the mourners to his final resting place. She watches the funeral director slowly lower his casket. The same way he watched her parents going into the ground. She throws a red rose on his casket at the bottom of his grave with a tight smile and walks away.

* * *

Patrick asks, "Mom, you killed all those people? How did you feel afterward? Did anyone find out you did it?"

Eighty-eight-year-old Majesty replies, "Yes. I killed all of them. I would do it all over again if I had to. I had a lot of nightmares. It gets better after a while." She sips her tea and continues, "No one found out, just Miss Mary, and I knew what happened that night. The training helped me a lot. I accomplished the task and was very careful." She puts her teacup down. Arthur, in a deep sleep, is snoring. "Babies, people will bring the worst out of you. They can turn you into a completely different person than you were ordained to be."

Madison chimes in, "Patrick, why are you interrupting Mom? Let her finish the story."

CHAPTER 8
Let Your Hair Down

I t's Friday night. Majesty's coworker Nordia has invited her to her birthday party. The event will be held at the Cactus International at 9 p.m. sharp. Majesty remembers the time written on the invitation. She rushes, overtaking vehicles. She speeds, driving recklessly on the highway. Trying to get to the event. She glimpses the clock on her dashboard: 8:50 p.m. "I am late," she says. Hurrying through the busy highway, her vehicle abruptly shuts off.

"Please send help, God, please send help," says Majesty in a prayerful voice. She sits in her car hoping someone can help her.

In her rearview mirror, she sees two figures approaching her. She reaches for her Glock, places it in her lap, and puts her jacket over it. The two men introduce themselves.

"Hi, are you OK?" asks the tall man.

Majesty replies, "The car suddenly shut off on me."

He commands, "Open the hood." The men talk among themselves. He speaks again. "I live in the area not too far from here."

She says, "OK." She opens the hood of her car. She is relieved to get the help and explains to the men what is happening to her vehicle. The men listen attentively and give their opinions on what they think the issue could be.

A few minutes later, a black BMW 5 Series stops in front of her parked car. Majesty doesn't know the driver. Somehow, she feels a sense of comfort.

I have company, she thinks to herself. *This person looks like they, too, are on their way to the Kingston area.*

Her thoughts are interrupted. Time stands still. A very attractive man exits the car. This man is about six feet tall. He has broad shoulders. The most perfect lips she has ever seen. His golden-brown eyes shimmer in the lights projecting from her headlamps. *He is perfect*! Majesty is at a loss for words. She stares that chocolate man down like a hungry beast.

The two men approach his car and start talking to him. He, too, is seemingly having car issues as he opens the hood of his car to observe his engine. He shifts his focus and starts to walk towards Majesty's car.

"Hi, are you OK?" he asks. His deep-toned voice makes her quiver!

"My car won't start." Majesty immediately goes into damsel-in-distress mode.

He asks her permission to examine her engine. She gladly says, "Yes." Once he is through, he figures that both cars are overheating. He tells the men to get two gallon bottles of water.

The two stand in silence as the men go to get the water. Their eyes speak for them. The gentlemen return with the water and pour it in both cars. Majesty turns her ignition on, and to her surprise, the car starts.

She is ecstatic. "Yes, thank you, God!" She says to the men, "Thank you."

She speeds off. What a night! She eyes her dashboard again. It's 10:48 p.m. She rushes to Nordia's party.

* * *

Three weeks later, Majesty is learning to have fun after the ordeal with Bob. She puts that life to rest. She starts enjoying life to the fullest. She loves the party scene and is very outgoing. One night, she has one of her party escapades. She is dancing and drinking with friends at a fashion show after-party. She receives a phone call. The music is loud. She is unable to hear the person on the other line. She steps out to accommodate the call.

She answers, "Hello, hey Nordia, how are you? Is everything OK?"

Nordia replies, "Can you pick me up from the airport tomorrow at 11 a.m.?"

Majesty says, "OK, I will be there."

"Cut the call," a deep voice shouts to her from behind. It sounds familiar, but she can't quite figure it out.

Then she turns and looks in the direction where the voice is coming from. It's the perfect golden-brown-eyed man she saw weeks ago when her car broke down on the dark highway. "Is this fate?" she asks herself.

After getting the details of Nordia's flight information, she ends the call. She walks over to his vehicle. He sits in his car with his hand out, gesturing to her.

"Hey, what's up? How have you been?" she asks.

He doesn't seem to recognize her. He is talking to her as if she is a total stranger. He praises her for her physique and her beauty. Majesty is a bit taken aback. She quickly cuts him off and asks, "Don't you remember me?"

He says, "No, should I?"

She says, "Remember that night on the highway we both got stranded?"

He is astonished, not remembering why he let her leave without giving him her phone number. Staring and convinced, saying, "Yes, it's you." They both laugh. "I never asked you your name. How rude of me," he says.

"Comala, but my close friends call me Majesty."

"That's a pretty name, Majesty."

"What is your name?" Majesty asks.

"Arthur."

Arthur seems to have an interest in Majesty. He asks, "Can we go somewhere quiet to get to know each other?"

She thinks to herself, *The party is a bit boring. What's the worst thing that can happen? I have my gun and can protect myself if he tries anything.*

She agrees. She tells him, "Give me a few."

She goes back inside and tells her friends she is leaving. She emerges. He is staring her down from head to toe. He says to himself, "This girl looks amazing. Wonder if she has a man." Talking to himself. "Well, if you do, I want you all for myself."

The two go to a restaurant nearby. The hostess greets them and leads them to a table for two. He pulls out her chair and says, "Ladies before gentlemen." He is so charming!

He says, "I want to get to know you, Comala, or should I call you Majesty? I like Majesty better. You are a queen."

She laughs sheepishly.

They spend the next few hours together, laughing and talking about their likes and dislikes. They are both lost in the moment.

He asks, "Do you have a man, Majesty?"

She wipes her lips with the napkin. She replies, "No." She quickly remembers Antwan, her first boyfriend. After Antwan migrated to Canada, she was caught up trying to kill Bob. Now that chapter of her life is over, she can enjoy the rest of her life.

After dinner, they exchange phone numbers and go in different directions.

At 8 a.m. the next day, her cellphone rings. When she looks at the screen, she sees it is Arthur calling.

"Hello, can I invite you out to lunch today?" the deep-toned voice asks.

She has never felt this way before for somebody. Excitedly, Majesty says, "Yes. I have a few errands to run, including picking a friend up from the airport. Any time after midday would be fine."

Majesty arrives at the airport. She is so happy to see Nordia. She says, "Girl, I met the most perfect man a few weeks ago. Rushing to your party. Remember I told you my car shut off on the highway? My knight in shining armor came and rescued me."

They both laugh. She continues, "The funny thing is we didn't exchange names. When my car started, I told him thanks and drove away. I saw him again at the party when you called. I stepped outside, and there he was, trying to get my attention. Isn't that weird?"

Nordia replies, "It's about time you finally like someone. I tried introducing you to James, Steven, and Matthew. You hated all of them. I hope this works out for you."

She says, "I am having lunch with Arthur after dropping you off."

Nordia fills her in on her trip as they sing the song on the radio.

Majesty wastes no time. She drops her friend off and heads for the restaurant. When she gets there, Arthur is already in the parking lot awaiting her arrival.

He steps out of the car to meet her. He is well-dressed and looks like the main course for the dinner they are about to have. He hugs her, and her nostrils are captivated by his Blee fragrance flying off him. She has no choice but to be drawn to him.

The lunch date is wonderful. They both laugh and chat until it's time to say goodbye.

He invites her out on a couple more other dates. They have a lot of fun hanging out together. One day, he tells her, "I am going back home to the United States in two weeks."

She is unhappy; she is just getting to know him and enjoying his company. She remembers her Grandma Merkle got her a visa so she could travel. She unreservedly responds, "I have a visitor's visa. I can visit you any time."

"That would be lovely," he says. It is a dream come true. She likes him. And he likes her too.

The following week, he invites her to the beach. He picks her up from her house and takes the winding road to Forum Beach. The sky and the gem-blue salty water connect with each other. She slips off her jeans and adjusts her red swimsuit. He is thrilled to see her physique. His undershirt rolls and reveals his muscular abs, and his swimming trunks hug his lean frame. She thinks to herself, *Looks like he works out.*

She says, "Arthur, let's get in the water." Her voice sends his senses on alert. He straightens his shoulders. She enjoys the adventure with her man. *I never imagined feeling so comfortable around someone. The butterflies in my stomach. I feel passion, kindness when he touches me,* she thinks.

Arthur holds her hand and takes her to the ocean floor. She spots a few pieces of seaweed at the surface. The warm water splashes against her face. Saltwater splashes in her mouth, hitting her taste buds. The screeching of birds fills the air. He lays her down to float on the water. She closes her eyes. The warm sunlight and clear water shimmer on her golden skin. The calm waves crawling gently to the shore. The sound echoes a plush rhythm. The cool ocean breeze blows a resinous aroma of clean, fresh air.

Arthur leans his body against hers. His breath caresses her body. All her muscles loosen up. He kisses her lips, and his lips end up on her neck. Majesty wraps her legs around his waist. Then he whispers in her ear, "Baby, you mean so much to me." She quickly realizes she is in trouble and peels herself away from him.

She says, "Arthur, I am not ready."

He replies, "I won't do anything you don't want to do. Whenever you are ready." He kisses her hand. He quickly splashes the water on her face, and they play like children in a playground.

The following week, he leaves Jamaica. Weeks go by without talking to him. She is missing him more with each passing day. One day, she gets a phone call from him. He laments about how much he misses her. It makes her feel wanted and loved. She is happy.

He asks, "Can you come and visit me? I miss you so much."

She replies, "Yes, Arthur. I miss you too. Why did you take so long to call me? I thought you forgot about me."

He speaks. "Baby, because I spend so much time in Jamaica. I had to get some business going. I can now relax after taking care of that. Sorry about that, my love. Can I book your flight for next week?"

Majesty loves him. She says, "Yes." This is the beginning of their story!

CHAPTER 9

The 95

"**W****elcome to the Norman Manley International Airport. Please secure your luggage. Do not leave your luggage unattended."**

This can be heard repeatedly over the intercom. Majesty anxiously waits to board her flight from Jamaica to Fort Lauderdale. The usual one-hour-fifty-eight-minute flight feels like five hours. Majesty thinks of how much she misses Arthur and cannot wait to see him.

Upon deplaning, she follows protocol and is processed by immigration. She is given six months in the country. She collects her luggage. Her mind is racing. Her heart is beating fast. Palms are sweating. "I am one step closer to seeing my baby," she thinks.

She retrieves her luggage and exits. Passengers are waiting with their suitcases. Others stand outside waiting to be picked up. The arrival entrance is busy as passing vehicles go to and from different gates. It seems Arthur is bubbling with excitement, too. He is already outside, eagerly waiting for her.

He is dressed in a white polo shirt, blue jeans, and white sneakers. He looks as though he is ready to be devoured. She feels a tingle she never felt before in her pussy. It is her first time feeling like this for a man. She was so caught up in wanting to kill Bob. A man was never on her mind. She has to clench her thighs to stop her natural juices from flowing. When he sees her, they embrace. He gently puts his hands around her. Sexual tension is rising. She can feel his member press against her belly button.

"How was your flight, baby?" he asks.

She replies, "Long, only because I couldn't wait to see you." They laugh.

He puts her luggage in his black BMW X5. He opens the passenger side door for her. They start their journey. Majesty doesn't care to ask where she is going. She is hot and bothered by Arthur. She is ready for the ride. Literally, anywhere is good enough as long as she is with him.

They drive for about five minutes, hand in hand, before merging onto the highway, the great Interstate 95. He pulls to the side of the road and leans in for a kiss.

They started to kiss passionately. His breathing increases. At this point, the juices Majesty tried hard to stop are flowing freely. They are both aroused and hungry for each other. Arthur's hard cock stands up in respect for the work of art he is dealing with. Though they are in a car on the side of the road, he wants to have her here and now. He forces her pants down. Without any reservations, she opens her legs wide for him, with each one extending to either side of the X5. "I can't believe I am having sex in a car, on the highway. In America," she says to herself.

Arthur seems to have not eaten for a few days. He must have been starving. He eats her pussy out like it is the first meal he has seen in days. He uses his fingers to make way for his meal. The moment he sees her pussy, he groans. At this point, Majesty is soaking wet. The juices from her pussy are already streaming down her inner thighs and soaking the leather interior of his car. He carefully uses his tongue in a circular motion to please her. He follows this pattern for a while, and the more he does it, the better it feels; he inserts a finger into her already waiting tight hole while still using his tongue to clean up any spills.

Majesty thinks to herself, when she first had sex with Antwan, it didn't feel like this.

When Arthur touches her, it is an unexplainable out-of-body experience. She moans in ecstasy. She calls his name, nearing climax. She screams! "Oh, fuck yes, baby, fuck!" She reaches her climax. She kisses

43

him passionately. She knows she has to please her man after the way he just made love to her.

Cars are busy passing, horns honking, but nothing matters. They are lost in time. Majesty gets to her knees on the passenger seat and takes his hard throbbing cock out of his pants. She holds it in her hands, examining it carefully while caressing it.

She knows she has to bring out her inner freak. She licks, spits, caresses, and sucks the life out of this man's body. She puts his dick in her mouth and sucks it. She can feel the tension building up. She uses her tongue to please him. He holds on to her head and forces his dick down her throat. Causing her to gag! She doesn't care. She wants more.

She mounts his dick. And boy, is it a perfect fit for her wet, tight pussy. She can feel her body submitting to him. She sits on his dick and rides him like a jockey on a horse. Beads of sweat build up as the sex gets intensified. After about ten minutes of pure riding. Arthur explodes inside of her. "Baby, this is what heaven feels like," he groans. He was too busy, quickly removing his shirt and cleaning her up. He asks, "Did you have fun?"

She replies, "Yes."

"Thank you for sharing that with me. I do appreciate it."

They both laugh. Breathing heavily, they both are obviously tired. They fix their clothes and proceed to the route. He holds onto her hand for the rest of the ride.

He whispers, "Majesty, I missed you so much. I'm so happy you came to see me."

She replies, "I missed you too. I am so happy to see you and feel you." They both smile.

When they get to his house, they both shower and make love while bathing.

He thinks to himself, *Something about this girl. I can't put my finger on it. Am I falling in love? Oh my God.*

He takes her to dinner. They have an amazing evening.

* * *

Arthur Bitting was born in Jamaica. He grew up with his parents. His mother worked at a hair salon as a hairstylist. His dad was a police officer. They didn't have much. They ensured their son got the best education.

At the age of 17, his parents sent him to visit his aunt in Miami, Florida, for the summer holiday. He enjoyed his time, met a woman named Britney, and courted her for a while.

The visits to Miami became more frequent. The relationship with Britney grew. They got married. She was a United States citizen. When it was time for him to return to Jamaica, she wanted him to stay.

She petitioned for him, and he received his green card.

Arthur worked two jobs at a restaurant, washing and cleaning for minimum wage. And at night, repacking shelves for a grocery store. He couldn't do anything extra other than pay their bills. He didn't take her out. He couldn't afford it.

He hated the job. Arthur had to do it to help offset the rent, the bills, and the apartment he rented with Britney. With external stressors, Britney started cheating on him with a man who could take her out to fancy restaurants and not complain about bills. When Arthur found out, he was devastated.

"I am trying my best to help pay the bills, and this is what you do to me," he says to Britney. "I guess my best isn't good enough." They fought. He ended the marriage. It was short-lived. They got a divorce two years into their marriage. They went their separate ways; she moved to South Carolina and got married to the man she was cheating with.

Arthur stayed in Miami. He continued working at the restaurant, and he filed for his citizenship. He was miserable and heartbroken. He worked both jobs; he could hardly pay his bills. He was overworked and got very little pay.

Little did he know, this was about to change. He met Labron White.

CHAPTER 10

High Grades

Labron was a marijuana dealer. A well-dressed, never-repeat-his-sneakers kind of a guy. He sold weed on the street at the restaurant in Miramar where Arthur worked.

Arthur needed extra money. He was behind on his bills. He worked every day. He was tired of overworked-underpaid-boss-disrespecting-you jobs. He was getting below minimum wage and could not maintain his basic lifestyle. He lost his wife to another man. From that day on, he aspired to do more. He didn't want that to ever happen to him again. He was eager to learn the drugs game.

Labron was a veteran in the business. He drove the latest cars. His swag was always on point. Always flashing coils of money. That impressed Arthur. Arthur was broke, and a dope man flashing money would motivate any individual. Arthur thought to himself, *All I need is a head start. I will sell some dime bags, save my money, and make something of myself.*

Arthur needed to learn what Labron was doing. Arthur was very organized and had leadership skills. His motto was "MY WORD IS MY BOND." He said what he meant and meant what he said.

Labron took Arthur under his wing and helped him get into the business. Labron wasted no time starting Arthur off on his first deal. "If

I have more manpower, I can make more money," Labron said to himself.

After selling dope for a month, Arthur tripled his pay. He worked less. He dressed nicely every day. Arthur quit the restaurant job. His life started to improve drastically.

Years later, Arthur and Labron still worked together. They mastered dime bags, working the street corners together. Arthur couldn't stop; he got accustomed to the lifestyle. He would never go back to dime bags. He was smart; he wanted to get to the next level. He studied the game and worked profusely. Arthur rose to boss status.

* * *

"Mom? Grandpa was a drug dealer. Our father was a drug boss? Why did you date him? You know that's what got your father killed," says Demetre.

Eighty-eight year-old Majesty answers, "Demetre, sometimes the past shapes the future. Take note:

"My father Dehon bought a house cash for his family. Working a minimum wage job, he couldn't purchase that home for my mother. He sold his soul for a house. And he lost his life.

"I was not looking for a drug boss. It just happened like that. Arthur worked two jobs. He still couldn't maintain his basic needs. His first wife left him. It was devastating for him, so he got in the game.

"Drug dealers think they can get rich overnight. Yes, that's true. But you can go to prison for a very long time or lose your life. Getting rich doesn't solve all their problems. In fact, in the drug game, you constantly watch for the police. Paranoia can set in. You are always looking over your back for thieves and so-called friends with the intention of setting you up to rob you. Most of these men went to school but didn't go to college to obtain degrees to get a career. They must work for minimum wages. Sometimes, two different jobs. Life can get frustrating. The risk and the penal punishment outcome can be very bad.

"Most of the time, drug dealers are willing to sacrifice themselves to give their family a better opportunity, example, They can afford to buy everything that life has to offer. But is it worth it?"

She continues with the story.

* * *

Arthur got so big in the game that he expanded beyond the corner of the street. Arthur and Labron started traveling all over the United States. Arthur helped Labron get more respect from the men they worked for. Arthur showed him how to save his money; he taught him to buy assets and support his family in Jamaica.

Arthur saved his money. He bought his own merchandise. He now supplied the men they were working for with better-quality weed. He purchased a home for his parents. It was during that trip that he met Majesty.

* * *

Arthur treats Majesty like royalty. He takes her shopping, to movies, and on expensive dinner dates. He takes her to see a Miami Heat basketball game. Arthur will not make that mistake twice, not taking out his lady. Majesty is having the time of her life. He takes her to meet his mother's sister. She lives not too far from where he lives in Pembroke Pines. They are enjoying every moment together.

Majesty has now been in Florida for over a week. She is getting ready to go back home. Her ticket is only booked for two weeks. Arthur is sad. He has made a connection with her. He doesn't want her to leave.

"Baby, we are having so much fun. Please don't leave me. I am going to New York. Do you want to come with me?" he asks.

This sounds very inviting. It would be her first time in New York. She wouldn't miss it for the world.

She says, "Yes. I would love to go with you." She calls Miss Mary and tells her she will stay longer on her trip.

Some of Arthur's family and friends live in New York. He is excited to have his family meet the new love of his life.

Arthur is always talking to his parents on the phone. He says to her, "I never hear you speak about your parents."

She answers, "When I was eight years old, I witnessed three men murdering my parents. The men set our home on fire. I was left to burn."

He is astonished to hear that. He can't think about being in that situation. He asks, "What happened to those men? Are they in jail?"

She replies, "They are all dead."

Her mind jogs back quickly to when she killed Bob. Tears fill her eyes. Arthur hugs her and comforts her. He sees an emotional side he has never experienced. Quickly, he changes the subject.

He says, "Let us watch a movie tonight. I will make the popcorn."

She says, "OK."

He introduces her to his parents on the phone. And his friends Alion, Lex, and Labron.

Arthur and Majesty have a whirlwind romance. They are two peas in a pod. They smoke weed together. Always dressing in similar-looking outfits. They look so cute together. "Inseparable" is an understatement.

Arthur books the Cool Shade Exclusive Suites in New York. Their room is in the penthouse. It is located on the 41st floor, overlooking the city skyline. It stretches from the east to the west. The beautiful light sparkles across the breathtaking city. The waterway is wide and deep. "This is amazing. Picture-perfect view," Majesty says.

Arthur's friends frequently visit him. They quietly talk about business. When his friends are there, Majesty goes on the balcony and admires the spectacular panoramic nightlife of the city.

She enjoys fine dining, shopping, and spending time with his family and friends. When the trip nears the end, Arthur asks, "Babe, I am going to Phoenix, Arizona. Can you come with me, pretty please?"

She answers, "Hell yes!" They both laugh hard.

Majesty cannot believe it. She is traveling to places she never thought she would go with the perfect man. Her life is a fairytale.

On the morning they leave for Phoenix, he hands her four wads of money. He says, "Put these in your four jeans pockets. Pack them away in your luggage. I have no more space to put them."

Puzzled, she looks at him. She does what she is told.

She can't contain her curiosity. She asks, "Where did you get all this money? Is this money legal?"

He smiles and says, "Baby, relax. I am a businessman. I am going to handle some business in Arizona."

She is madly in love with him. She doesn't even care about the details of the money. Legal or not, she is going to do what she needs to do to be with him.

They land in Phoenix. The flight and immigration proceedings are seamless. Arthur makes reservations for a luxury vehicle before landing. His organizing skills are second to none. He ensures he rents a townhouse. Upon exiting the airport, he collects the keys to the car. He drives to their rented home for the duration of their stay.

They pull up to a gated community. He gives the guard his credentials. In exchange, he hands him the house keys. Arthur is very meticulous in how he handles his business. He enters through the garage for very specific reasons. It is beautiful, she thinks.

* * *

Alion McKenzie was born in New York to Jamaican parents. As a teenager, his parents would take him to visit his grandparents in Jamaica for the summer holidays. It was on one of those trips that he met Labron and Lex.

He lived in New York and struggled to make ends meet. He worked so many dead-end jobs for very little pay. He was so frustrated. His last 9-to-5 job was at a used car dealership. He learned how to hustle. It was a commission-based paying job. He had to make sure he was selling as many vehicles as possible to meet his quota to break even or make a bonus at the end of the month. With that experience, he was inspired to one day own a car dealership.

Over time, he started to slack off. Alion was not performing, so he got fired from the dealership.

After struggling to pay his rent, he was left with no choice but to rob other people just to maintain his basic lifestyle. He got so frustrated. He reached out to his longtime friend Labron. He knew the influence he had in the streets. He heard Labron took the game to another level. Alion needed an opportunity to make a better way of life.

Alion dialed Labron's phone number. Labron plucked the phone out of his pocket. He glanced to see if he recognized the name. Labron answered, "Hey, Alion," putting the phone on speaker and placing it in his lap, keeping his eyes on the road while talking.

Alion replied, "Labron, how are you? It's been a long time since I've talked to you." He continued, "I am not doing well over here. I need to work with you. I can't keep doing this. I robbed a man last night and shot him for nickels and dimes. I need an opportunity."

Labron replied, "OK. Let me talk to Arthur." He turned right. Keeping his eyes glued to the road, he continued, "Alion, I am doing very well. I just bought my mother a nice house in Jamaica. I have lots of big plans for myself. Arthur helps me. I would still be selling dime bags on the street corner. Arthur studies the hustle game. He put us in a better situation. He changed the trajectory of our life. That's why I respect him."

He made a right and continued, "I will call you later. And let you know what he says." He hung up the phone.

Labron made the connection. A few days later, Alion arrived in Arizona. One afternoon, Arthur, Labron, and Alion were on the road buying weed from their Mexican supplier.

Arthur went into the back and paid the Amigo mob boss. Alion and Labron packed eight garbage bags of weed in the cargo van that Arthur had rented.

Arthur said, "Let's go." One of the Mexican men slid open the big white gate. Arthur drove out. Labron and Alion sat in the back, securing the merchandise.

Arthur drove three miles. He stopped at a stop light. Two armed men pulled up in a black cargo truck. The taller man came out holding guns pointed at Arthur and commanded him, "Turn off the engine. And put your hand on the steering wheel." The shorter man went to the passenger side door, pointing his gun.

Alion and Labron appeared from nowhere, firing shots at both men and hitting the tall man; he fell to the ground. Alion went over to him and put three shots in his chest, killing him on the spot. Labron pointed his weapon at the shorter thief. Alion pushed him to the side of the truck. He opened the van and summoned him to get in. The man was so frightened he dropped his gun and did as he was told.

Arthur quickly drove away, parked in an empty parking lot, and got in the back of the van.

Alion beat the thief and asked, "Who sent you?" The man wasn't talking, so Alion dragged him out of the truck and blew his brains out.

Arthur was impressed. *This dude is so cold,* he thought to himself. *It's the hunger in him. The way Alion protected the merchandise with no fear. I can definitely use Alion's help in building the empire.*

Over time, Alion proved himself to be a loyal and dangerous soldier. The rest of the story is history. They went out of town regularly. They packaged containers of illegal substances and shipped them all over the States a few months at a time. After each shipment, they laid low for a while and repeated the cycle. They were making thousands of dollars without a glitch in the system. Everything was always smooth and going according to plan.

They kept a very tight circle.

Alion talked to Arthur about bringing in Lex to the crew. He said, "We need the extra hand. He can help with pickup."

Arthur was the boss; he ensured everyone in his circle was well taken care of. He rented private planes and bought homes and cars for everyone. He made sure their families were OK. He knew once his army was good, he was good.

Once they worked, they never had a problem getting their money. Arthur was always on point; he was big on loyalty and respect. After the weed shipped, they returned to Florida.

CHAPTER 11
Arizona

Arthur is in love with Majesty. He makes her feel safe and secure. He informs her of his moves and any changes he is making, without giving away too much information about what he is doing.

The couple makes love twice daily. They go on shopping sprees as often as they can. She is having the time of her life with him.

Arthur says, "Baby, my friends will be coming over here to help me with some business. They will be staying with us on the first floor. We have enough space and bedrooms."

She replies. "OK. When are they coming?" He replies, "Next week."

A few days later, Alion, Lex, and Labron arrive at the house in Phoenix. When they arrive, they have a good time. They go to Phoenix Sun basketball games, clubbing, dinner, and bars and play pool. It is a great experience getting to chill with them and have fun with his friends.

One morning, she is awakened by a familiar but illegal scent. She is Jamaican. She knows the scent of weed like the back of her hand. It is coming from the living room. She marches down the stairs, and to her surprise, Arthur, Lex, Labron, and Alion are seated on the floor.

Lex is weighing and passing the merchandise to Alion. He is packing the weed in the boxes. Labron seals the boxes. Arthur labels the finished product.

They are surrounded by labeled packages. Compressed cannabis all over the living room.

The boxes are ready for delivery. The once clean and tidy house is filled with illegal substances. The packages have random names and addresses going all over the States.

The entire living room had approximately twenty large black trash bags of marijuana.

Majesty is startled. "Arthur, what the hell is this?"

He comforts her by saying, "Baby don't worry, this is what I do for a living. I have been doing this for years. It's OK."

She cannot believe her eyes. "This is the same thing that got my parents killed." She thinks, *how could she have missed it?* The money, the cars, the constant trips, the luxury brands.

"Fuck you, Arthur. You didn't give me an opportunity to choose if this is OK. What the fuck?"

She storms back upstairs. Feeling betrayed and feeling like an idiot.

He follows behind her. He says, "Majesty, calm down, this is safe. I have been doing this for years. My team works very clean. This is what we do for a living. This is the way we transport the products across the country. The delivery driver. The shipping agents are all working for me. I got this baby. Just trust me. I have my connections in every examination point. Trust me. We're good!" He continues, "Just rest your pretty head, baby. Pick out a sexy outfit for dinner. I will make it up to you."

It takes Majesty a while to come to terms with the fact that she is in love with a drug dealer. She says, "Arthur, I lost my parents when I was eight years old. My father sold dime bags of weed for a lowlife. This man named Bob and two of his friends came to my home one night and murdered my parents. Then burned my house down. I saw everything through my door. If they saw me, they would've killed me, too. I had to escape through my window. It is very hard for me; I don't want to lose you. I am in love with you."

He hugs and kisses her and wipes her tears. He promises that this is very safe. She calms down. He goes back to finish putting the labels on the boxes.

Marijuana is illegal, but she is starting to enjoy the lifestyle. She is head over heels for Arthur. She admires the way he delegates and gets things done. He is the boss, and that is sexy. She watches them work. Seeing it gives her unspeakable joy. Her man is in charge. Majesty starts to feel sick, especially in the mornings. She is nauseated. She is sleeping all the time. She loses her appetite. She tries to convince herself that the weed in the house may be strong. It's making her feel this way.

* * *

One morning, Arthur wakes her up with a kiss. He says, "I am going to do a delivery with Labron. I will go to the gym after the drop-off and work out."

"OK, boo."

"We will be back a little late today. Call me when you wake up."

She blankly responds, "OK." When she finds the urge to get up, she eventually goes downstairs. Alion, Lex, and Alion's girlfriend, Roxanne, are watching TV. She sits with them and chit-chats for a bit. She begins to feel nauseous and sleepy again, so she goes back upstairs to bed.

About an hour after resting, she hears screaming sirens coming in their direction. When she peeps through the window blinds, she sees about seven flashing police cars surrounding the road and driveway and about ten uniformed police officers approaching the house. It reminds her of when the police came to her house in Jamaica when her parents were murdered.

She thinks to herself, *Oh shit! The house is loaded with illegal guns and high volumes of marijuana. Oh my God.*

She runs downstairs to tell the others what she has seen. Lex and Alion are already aware. They are on their way upstairs. Trying to get rid of any evidence that can incriminate them. Alion is flushing bands of money down the toilet and breaking up their phones.

Alion's girlfriend, Roxanne is there with Alion flushing money in the other bathroom. She is panicking and praying, asking God to keep her safe because she is illegal and has two other offenses against her. She is undocumented in the country; she knows she will be deported if she were to be connected with any more criminal activities.

Majesty tries to call Arthur's cellphone; it rings without an answer. She tries repeatedly and gets no answer.

She knows there is no way to escape this, and jail is inevitable. What the fuck did she get herself into?

She returns to her bedroom and puts on jeans, a warm shirt, socks, and a sweater.

She grabs her passport and shoves it into her back pocket. She then packs her stuff in a suitcase and thinks quickly about her next move.

She keeps calling Arthur, but there is no answer. With little time to spare, she brushes her hair in a ponytail and goes back down the stairs, walking into the predictable.

Alion is so nervous he is pacing back and forth.

Lex is nowhere to be found. "Where is Lex?" she asks.

Alion replies, "He got scared, and jumped out the window."

"What?" she replies. "Lex jumped from a three-story building."

She runs to the window and looks down at Lex's lifeless body splattered on the ground in the bushes. There is blood everywhere. She covers her mouth and shouts, "Alion, Lex is dead. He is not moving!" Her voice is shaking.

Alion and Roxanne rush over to the window and stare at him. Alion says, "Oh shit," and shakes his head. He continues, "OK, listen up, let's get rid of all his paperwork so he has no connection with us."

The sirens are screaming at the front of the building. Alion continues speaking. "We cannot let them know we know him." Alion rushes to Lex's bedroom, runs through his suitcase, takes out his documents with his name on them, and destroys them. "Let's close the window blinds and pretend it's just us staying here. It's a good thing it's just bushes back there." Alion looks scared of what's going to happen to them. He isn't even thinking about Lex at that moment.

One of the police officers says on a loudspeaker, "This is the Phoenix Police Department. We have you surrounded. Come out with your hands on your heads right now before we break down the door."

Alion comes up with a story. No one is blinking.

"OK. We will tell the cops that I met you and Roxanne at the club last night, and I offered for you, Majesty, to stay with me at this apartment. Just put all the blame on me." His voice is calm and direct.

"Don't talk about Arthur, Lex, or Labron. It's just us. You got it?" His eyes flicker down. He continues speaking. "Majesty, let them know you are visiting from Jamaica. You were staying at Homes Sweet Home Hotel. It became too expensive. You are running out of money, hence why you are here. Roxanne, tell them you met Majesty at the club, and both came to see me." They all agree and decide to corroborate the story.

Majesty thinks to herself, *Alion is very brave. He has loyalty and integrity.*

CHAPTER 12
Getting Caught

lion reiterates, "No matter what, DO NOT CHANGE THE STORY. Girls, this is going to be crazy. Don't fold. If it gets bad, ask for an attorney. Just keep the same story and be calm. Let's go down now before they break the door down."

Alion shouts, "I have no weapon. We are coming down the stairs one by one." They put their hands on their heads and trail down the stairs as they were ordered. The police point their guns at them as they slowly march in a line.

Alion is first, followed by Majesty and Roxanne. Majesty scans the area. The duty officers, dressed in their police uniforms, have their guns pointed in their direction.

When they get outside, the police move in on them like a swarm of bees. One of the officers puts handcuffs on each of them. They order Majesty to sit on the concrete opposite Roxanne and Alion. The lead detective asks, "Is anyone else in the house?"

Alion answers, "No."

Majesty cannot help but think about Lex's lifeless body.

The police go in without showing them a warrant and start to search the house. They don't even read them their rights. They just continue with their business, making trips in and out, taking bags of evidence.

Majesty knows it is the end for her. She thinks, *My parents must be rolling in their graves right now. I can't believe I let Miss Mary, Merkle, Kester, Wilma, and Septemus down. The American dream. Getting caught up in illegal activities. Now facing time behind bars.* It feels like a terrible nightmare from which she wants to wake up.

Alion, Roxanne, and Majesty are placed in the back of three cars and taken to jail.

When they arrive at the police station, they are all taken into different private rooms for interrogation. They all must maintain the same story.

Two police officers are in the room with Majesty. They question her. "Do you live at that house?"

She replies, "No. I am on vacation. I was staying at the Home Sweet Home Hotel. I was running out of money. I went to the club, and I met Roxanne and Alion. He offered for us to stay with him last night. When I woke up, I heard the police siren," Majesty explains. The situation reminds her of Constable Mills talking to her after her parents' murder.

The female cop asks, "Did you know the house was filled with so much contraband?"

She says, "No."

The male police officer asks, "Tell me again from start to finish how you got there."

Majesty holds on to her story. She has been in this situation before. She relays to the officers what she had corroborated with Alion.

The police are persistent and find different ways to ask her the same questions. She keeps a straight face and maintains her initial answer.

The interrogation prolongs; Majesty begins to get uneasy. She is hungry and tired and cannot help but wonder if Arthur is safe. The officers check her into Agusta Jail. She will be held until further notice. She doesn't see Alion or Roxanne. Majesty is told that she will be seen by a judge within the next 24 hours to determine her bail bond.

* * *

As Majesty walks down the hallway of the jail, she feels an eerie, cold feeling. Sounds of females arguing, laughing, and making inappropriate remarks at her. It is the longest walk of her life. The policewoman places her in a small cage. There is no freedom, no space to breathe. It has a flat, hard bed and a metal lavatory that is all in sight.

Tired, afraid, and worried, Majesty attempts to rest on her rock-hard bed. Her mind is like a maze. Thoughts are scrambling to find a place in her head, trying to calm her anxiety. *Lex got paranoid and jumped. Oh boy.* She shakes her head. *I hope Roxanne won't get deported! I know Alion can take care of himself. He is a good soldier. But most importantly, where the hell is Labron and my man?* Drained from her own thoughts. Majesty falls asleep.

She has a dream. She dreams of her parents walking in a beautiful field of flowers, telling her they are proud of her and how much they love her. This is the first time she has seen her parents in a dream. She doesn't want to wake up.

That dream is short-lived as she is awakened by a guard who greets her by saying, "Get up, Barbie, the judge is ready for you."

The guard is beautiful; she is tall and dressed in a khaki uniform with a neat ponytail. Her facial features indicate that she has been in this profession for a while and is slowly aging, possibly due to the stressful nature of the job.

The guard gestures to Majesty to position herself to be cuffed. She obliges.

As she stumbles through the hallway with her hands cuffed behind her, she sees a closed door with "Judge Lindsay" written on the nameplate.

The guard knocks, and a stern voice from inside says, "You may enter."

The judge is sitting on the podium. She is clad in a black gown. She sports a short pixie cut and has very manly shoulders, maybe from working out. She has a serious disposition, and you can tell she is a no-nonsense person. She has a gavel in her hand as she reads from a file.

Majesty tries to hold a straight face and reminds herself to stick to the same story.

The judge asks her, "What is your name?"

"Comala Facey, your honor," she responds.

"Where do you live?" asks the judge.

"Jamaica, your honor," she replies.

The judge then reads her the charges out loud. They are as follows:

"Illegal possession of a firearm, trafficking dangerous drugs and money laundering." The judge then asks, "How do you plead, guilty or not guilty?"

Majesty is resolute in her response. "Not guilty."

"Very well, then your bond is set at fifty-four hundred dollars. I will see you back in thirty days."

Majesty is dismissed. The clerk of courts hands her a disposition paper with the charges, the bond amount, and booking number.

She thinks to herself, *How the hell I am going to get out of this situation now? Arthur wasn't picking up when I called? Who is going to bail me out?* She walks out of the bail hearing, feeling defeated and powerless. How does one go from having everything they could ever need to absolutely nothing?

Inmates are not allowed to remain in their personal clothing. Majesty, now a prisoner, is no exception to the rule. The guard gives her a bag with a striped uniform, undershirt, panties, socks, and a pair of slippers. "You will now take a shower." She is led to the bathroom, where she is instructed to remove her clothing and place it in a bag. Again, she obliges.

She can't hold back the tears from rolling down her face while showering in the seemingly public restroom. It has eight shower stalls with no privacy in sight.

She whispers a prayer to herself, "Lord, I promise if you get me out of this, I will do your will." She showers and reassures herself of her name and how powerful it is. She whispers, "My name is MAJESTY. This is mind over matter. I got this." She knows she has to find a way to be strong!

The guard takes the bag with her personal belongings and hands her a blanket. "Here this is your disposition letter. It has all the charges. Keep it safe; recite your number. In this jail, you are referred to by your number, not your name," says the guard. Majesty scans the paper to check out the number: 34675-058. They walk for about three blocks before they get to Block B. She resides on the second floor in jail cell #23.

In this jail cell, the light is bright, and the room is cold; it is bigger than the holding jail cell she was in when she first got arrested. It has a bunk bed, a toilet, and a tiny window all the way to the top of the roof. Majesty is convinced the purpose of the window is only so you can see if it is day or night. She thinks to herself, *I am in a vicious cycle without revolution.*

In her cell is a beautiful, long-haired, petite Hawaiian girl. She cannot be more than 24 years old. She says, "Hi, I am Stephany."

"Hello, I am Majesty." Stephanie is so pleasant. Without even asking, she offers Majesty the top bunk.

The bunkies start to interrogate each other regarding their reasons for being in lockup and if they have bail, etc. "How much is your bail?" asks Stephany.

"Fifty-four hundred dollars," says Majesty.

Stephany is speechless. "What the fuck did you do? Did you kill somebody?"

"No," Majesty responds blankly. "I was at the wrong place, at the wrong time. Why are you here?" a curious Majesty asks.

"Some guy raped me, and I stabbed him in the chest," Stephany explains. "The guy is rich, so the police locked me up instead of him." She swears she will kill him if she ever gets released.

CHAPTER 13

Riot

The clanking of the utensils being used by the kitchen staff and the indistinct chatter of the inmates are buzzing through the hallways of the cafeteria.

Majesty has been in jail for well over five hours, and it is time to eat. She and her newfound friend Stephany make their way down to have dinner.

This setting is foreign to Majesty. Waiting in line to get food, everyone uniformed in black and white striped jumpers, socks, and slippers, not having access to any cutlery for safety purposes. This has to be a sick joke!

The place is very orderly, or so it seems. You have to form a queue to be served. You don't have a choice as you wait for your turn. The inmates form a straight line, and they have to collect a tray at the beginning of the line, on which their food is placed.

The servers have a mean, mugging look on their faces. They seem to have served time and are angry at the system, so they have no joy in their job. As Majesty approaches the server, a large brown slab of something is placed on her plate. She tries to figure out if it is meat, cardboard, or just a brown slab of nothing. It looks disgusting! They had the audacity to add vegetables to it, also a mini box milk, bread, and a banana to make it a "balanced meal."

All Majesty can do is reminisce on the times when she went to the top restaurants for steak and lobster, sipping pinot grigio and some strawberry cheesecake.

After collecting their food, Stephany and Majesty make their way to where they have decided to sit. There are two other females already seated at the table, so they exchange pleasantries and begin to eat their meal.

Stephany glimpses in Majesty's direction. Stephany notices Majesty's reaction to the food and tells her, "Don't worry, you will get used to it, but girl, you better eat, 'cause trust me! You will need your strength in this hell hole!"

Majesty forces a smile. Talk about the power of the tongue.

Not long after, a group of girls approaches their table. The "leader," Alicia, is tattooed all over her body. It is clear she is in charge, the way she walks in the front, and everyone else follows. She approaches Majesty without any regard for the others. The other inmates already know this is how she operates. In a commanding tone, Alicia asks, "What are you here for?"

Majesty answers, "That's none of your business," with a smirk on her face and looks her up and down. It reminds her of when Kendon Gardon used to bully her in school. *Who does this bitch think she is talking to?* Majesty thinks.

Alicia is taken aback, and so she gets closer. Alicia is locked up for two years for robbing a bank. She got caught, and her cousin, who was with her, got killed. She is awaiting sentencing to be shipped off to prison to serve her time. She bullies every new inmate; once she gets under their skin, she has them braiding her hair, folding her clothes, and getting her meals. She believes she owns everyone.

Alicia is so close to her face Majesty can smell her bad breath.

"Bitch, this is my territory, and whatever I say goes in here," Alicia says in an intimidating voice.

Everyone is surprised, quiet, and anxious to see her response. Majesty already knows how to deal with bullies. And her training she had all those years, preparing for Bob helps. This girl doesn't know how dangerous she can get. Majesty hates to get to this dark place that is now overtaking her.

Majesty stands up looks her straight in her eyes, and asks her, "What is it to you, and by the way, did you brush your stink breath this morning?" Trying to embarrass her, in a sarcastic voice. Alicia feels like Majesty is trying to upstage her, especially on her turf. Alicia slaps Majesty in the face. Majesty punches her in the nose and kicks her in her crotch; she falls on the floor. Majesty jumps on top of her and squeezes her neck with all her might. Alicia's eyes roll back, and she is about to lose consciousness.

Majesty says in a demanding voice, "Don't you ever talk to me like that ever again. I will kill you bitch. Do you know who you're playing with?" Alicia's eyes are widened in fright; she is in shock.

The dining area is suddenly transformed into a jungle, with women fighting, scratching, pulling hair, screaming, and biting each other. Stephany stands her ground. She stays loyal to her new friend Majesty; after all, Majesty is the only person to stand up to this bitch, Alicia. Stephany throws a few punches at Alicia's followers.

It is pure chaos in the cafeteria. A guard is shouting over the intercom, "Stop fighting, or you will be placed in the hole." The other guards rush in, trying to get some form of order and prevent the fight from escalating any further.

They drag Stephany and Majesty away from the other girls and escort them in different directions.

Alicia is angry that someone stood up to her. On her way out, she shouts at Majesty and says, "I will catch you some other time bitch."

Majesty doesn't say a word. She gestures with a middle finger and smiles.

Stephany suffered a bruised lip, but she doesn't care. She respects Majesty for the bold move she made and starts to view Majesty in a different light. "OK, so she is a gangster! She is bad. She knows how to throw a fist. That's why her bail money is so high!"

No one can come close to Majesty after that; Stephany ensures she is protected. She protects her like she is her boss.

From that day on, Alicia is quiet; she stays in her lane and looks the other way when she sees Majesty coming in her direction.

Later that night, Stephany shares her story with Majesty. "I was molested as a child, and I killed my uncle who did it. My best friend Kirk hid the weapon and covered for me so I wouldn't get in trouble. Kirk is the sweetest." She smiles at the thought of Kirk. She continues, "I then met this rich man. He had everything. He took me out on expensive dates and treated me like a princess. I thought he loved me, but one night he took me to a party on his yacht. Some of his rich friends were there, and they all ran a train on me. When they satisfied themselves, I got hold of a knife and stabbed the shit out of one of the motherfuckers, but I am poor, and he is rich, so I got into trouble for protecting myself."

Tears are now flowing freely as she remembers the night it happened. "Kirk is the only one who knew that my uncle was sexually abusing me and what this rich man did too," she continues while wiping her tears.

"I had to steal to eat. This is why I have been in here so long. I have no family, no friends, nobody to bail me out, and my bail is only a thousand dollars!"

Majesty is sympathetic. "Stephany, I am so sorry to hear what you have been through." She says, "Stephany, I lost my parents when I was eight years old. And there's a possibility I might be pregnant." Majesty still doesn't mention why she is locked up.

Stephany replies, "I am sorry you lost your parents at a young age. Congrats on the pregnancy if you are." They both laugh.

She is in jail for about a week, still having feelings of nausea, missing Arthur with each passing day, and has a very loyal roommate.

The routine becomes monotonous. Get up, shower, have breakfast, exercise, cell, lunch, cell, dinner, shower, cell. There is not much to do.

One morning, she is awakened by her roommate, who is frantically shaking her. "What is your number?"

Majesty is irritated. "Girl, I am sleeping, and you wake me to ask me for my number?" Hesitantly, she reads the numbers to her.

"The guard called your number over the intercom, sis. You should roll up."

"Roll up?" asks Majesty. "What the hell is a roll up?"

Stephany says, "You're leaving."

Majesty is in disbelief. She starts to shake the cell and tries to get the attention of a guard. "Guard, guard!" she screams.

The same guard from her court day is the same person who shows up. Majesty asks, "Did you call my number over the intercom?"

"What is your number?" she asks in a familiar voice.

"34675-058," Majesty recites.

The guard says, "Yes, someone bailed you. Pack your stuff, and let me take you to the processing area."

Majesty is happy. She packs and is ready to go.

It is bittersweet for Stephany. She misses her friend already but is happy that Majesty gets to go home.

They share a bond, and Majesty makes her a promise. "Don't worry, I got you."

The processing department involves a lot of fingerprinting, signing documents, and more. She is happy to follow through the process; after all, she is going home.

She receives all her belongings and is given a disposition letter outlining her charges and court date.

She hasn't seen her passport in so long. She examines it to ensure it is hers and in tip-top shape. After satisfying herself, she shoves it into her back pocket and exits the building.

Once she is outside, she turns on her cellphone. It is going off! She has about eight missed calls and messages, none from Arthur. He is the first person she wants to hear from.

She quickly dials his number, and it goes straight to his voicemail.

She then calls Labron. It's the same thing. There is no answer. Alion broke his phone, so she doesn't bother to call him.

Something isn't right. Who bailed her out?

CHAPTER 14
Reunited

Fresh air is good! To see something other than the four walls of her cell is good. Still unknown to her who bailed her, Majesty sits outside the jail waiting for about one hour to see if anyone will pick her up. A white minivan pulls up. She looks at the driver; it's Arthur!

Her man has come to get her. She is happy! Not for one moment did she think her man would let her down.

She runs to him and embraces him tearfully. She wraps her legs around him, and they kiss passionately.

He asks her, "Majesty, are you OK?"

She replies, "NO! I am not OK. I have been here for over three weeks. I have been in a fight. I couldn't reach you by phone. And don't get me started on the food." Even though she missed him, she is angry at the series of events.

He says, "Baby, I am so sorry! I should have never dragged you into this. It is my fault."

She dismisses him quickly and asks, "Did you get arrested?"

He shakes his head. "The police followed Labron and me to the shipping store and waited until we completed the transaction. They arrested both of us."

She hands him the disposition paper she received. He reads it aloud and tells her he got similar charges.

He tells her, "The cops were watching the house for a while. That's how they caught us-"

Majesty cuts him off. She speaks. "Do you know that Lex is dead? He got paranoid and jumped through the window. Before the police raided the house. We didn't say anything to the cops. It's not listed on the charges that I am charged for."

He says, "I thought he got arrested with everyone." He looks around hoping she is pulling his leg. He continues, "How can this be, Majesty? Please tell me you are joking right now."

"Arthur, why would I be joking about Lex like that?"

She continues, "I don't know if his body is still in the same place. I think we should go check if they pick him up. If the police didn't, his body must be decomposing."

He says, "I got out a few hours ago. I was worried about you. I bailed you first. I know you're not used to being in this kind of situation."

He leads her to the passenger side of the vehicle and opens her door. "Get in," he says.

"I will bail Alion, then Labron the following day. I am trying to get all the money from the weed we sent out. We can get a lawyer to help us with our case. I must tell you, though, we cannot go back to the apartment since the police are holding it for evidence."

She asks, "Are we going to leave Lex there?"

For the first time, Arthur seems scared. He doesn't have things under control. He has bags under his eyes; he looks tired. The attractive Arthur she came to know is now overwhelmed, weary, and vulnerable. They drive off, and he holds her hand. Both unsure and afraid, they offer some comfort to each other.

He changes the subject. "What do you want to eat, baby?"

"Anything is better than what they give us to eat in that jailhouse."

They both laugh.

He takes her to a restaurant, and they order grilled salmon with garlic mashed potatoes and ginger ale. It's unlike Majesty to order a ginger ale unless she is hungover from the night before. She barely touches her food.

The little she ate, she has to excuse herself to the bathroom to throw up. She barely has an appetite.

"Are you OK, Majesty?" a concerned Arthur asks.

"I'm fine," she responds.

"You don't look too fine to me. Talk to me, baby. Maybe you got sick and caught something while you were in lockup," he says.

It was hard enough being locked up for both of them. With his finances now being questioned, how could she burden him with another responsibility?

Reluctantly, she says, "Arthur, I think I might be pregnant."

He smiles and says, "I know, I can feel it. Don't worry about it, baby. We will get through this together."

He hugs her tightly, and they have the food packed to go.

He stops at a dollar store to pick up a few personal items they may need just to get through.

He speaks. "We must be careful when we go back to the house. If someone sees us, we can be facing additional charges. We wait until Labron and Alion get bail. We'll go in the nighttime when everyone is asleep."

He takes her to a smaller two-bedroom unit on the other side of town and tells her, "This is where we will be staying until their next court date."

They both undress and proceed to the shower. The water is steaming hot. They want to wash away any memory of being in jail. They also want to love each other.

He takes her on a sexual journey in the shower. The glass doors are covered in mist, Majesty clinging for life as Arthur bends her over and inserts his hard throbbing cock inside of her. She lifts her leg for easier access.

The food she received in the jailhouse was insipid, and she didn't have an appetite for her Salmon, but she is hungry for Arthur. With the water beating on their backs, they enjoy each other until they reach their climax.

She returns most of the calls she missed while she was locked up. She tells everyone her phone was lost and she is just retrieving the numbers. She doesn't want them to be worried about her, nor does she want to be seen as a fool for getting involved in what she is involved in.

Later that night, she has a conversation with Arthur. Majesty shares her experience inside and tells him about her friend Stephany. She asks him to assist her in bailing her out once things are settled and everyone in his camp is out. Arthur agrees.

Over the next couple of days, Alion and Labron get bailed as Arthur promised. They all give an account of what happened. Roxanne is being held in an immigration holding facility awaiting deportation.

At 1 a.m. that pitch-black night, they drive back to the house and go to the back of the building. An unpleasant smell like spoiled meat and rotten eggs hangs in the air. Lex's remains are clearly still there.

They sneak into the house and grab a couple of garbage bags, shovels, a broom, cleaning products, and a bottle of water.

Labron grabs the flashlight. They quietly scoop up what is left of his body in a doubled garbage bag. They quickly place his remains in the truck. Arthur and Alion clean the area with soap and water.

"What a coward! I can't believe this man, even a woman stands on her ten toes, took it like a G, and held it better than he did, and the funny part of it is, he had a box of weed for himself sent to New York," Arthur says in an angry tone. "Guys, this is not the ideal situation, but it has to be done this way. We cannot get caught with this body. They will charge us with additional murder charges. We must bury him."

He drives on a long, twisting path. The beam of light passes until it becomes lonely, with no sign of life or buildings, just bushes and a dark path.

Arthur drives off the road and drives a mile in the dark bushes. Majesty says, "Stop here. We can bury him here."

Labron and Alion take the garbage bags out of the truck, and Arthur takes the shovels out. They all start digging. They dig for two hours and place his remains in the hole. They cover his remains with dirt. Majesty says a prayer. They discard the shovels. And they drive off. They all are so tired, hungry, and dirty.

Arthur reassures everyone everything will be OK.

The following morning. Arthur is constantly on his phone. He has a notepad, jotting things down. He is back in business, back to being in charge. He is trying to retrieve his money and giving the people on the other end of the phone instructions on where to send it.

Later that evening, he takes the disposition letters from Alion, Labron, and Majesty. He notices all the charges are similar and decides to call the best criminal lawyer in Phoenix. He schedules an appointment with the attorney's receptionist.

On the morning of the appointment, they drive about 45 minutes to see the lawyer. Arthur is wearing a blue shirt and pants; he looks sharp and smart. Majesty is dressed in a baby blue dress. You can smell the cologne from a mile away. Arthur has a briefcase closely secured in his left hand, and Majesty holds onto his right hand.

They enter the elevator to the 18th floor, Suite #567. Arthur knocks on the door, and a young lady, nicely dressed, opens the door. She leads them to the lounge and tells them Attorney Maynard will be with them shortly. Shortly after, the nicely dressed young lady emerges and leads them to the attorney's office. From the looks of things, this attorney is well accomplished. His office is on the 18th floor, and the view is breathtaking. His office is well-decorated. The hardwood floors, lilac-painted walls, and neatly organized bookshelf say a lot. All his accolades and accomplishments are brandished on the wall.

Arthur introduces Majesty as his fiancé and hands him the disposition letters. The attorney has a stern look on his face. It is clear he means business. He tells him the fees to process all four cases is $50,000.

Arthur opens the briefcase, displaying the cash. With just eye contact, they both understand each other.

He says, "I will research the arresting reports. I will get back to you. Give me a few days."

Arthur asks, "How much jail time are we looking at?" He looks in her direction. "Comala, who is a visitor, what's the worst thing that can happen?"

He replies, "Twenty-five years, and Comala will spend at least ten years in federal prison and get deported back to her birth country after she serves her time."

Majesty takes a deep breath. They are very optimistic about their fate. This can change the dynamic of their future.

After the meeting, they go for dinner, to clear their minds.

It is stressful, and there is no way to get out of this. The evidence is clear, and all the weapons and all the cash they found. Majesty asks, "What if I go back home? What will happen?"

Arthur replies, "They will extradite you. Then, after serving your time, deport you."

When they return to the house, Arthur tells Labron and Lex what the lawyer said. They all are fretting and worrying about what their fate will be.

Majesty is trying to be brave for everyone. Letting them know what is to be must be. "Let's just pray and let it work itself out."

The court day is fast approaching. Everyone is worried. They all are awaiting a very important phone call from the lawyer. Everyone is on edge, hoping for some good news. But doubtful at the same time.

The phone rings. Majesty answers, "Hello." The others listen keenly.

"Yes, this is Comala Facey. To whom am I speaking?" She continues. She listens attentively. Alion, Labron, and Arthur are sitting anxiously, biting their nails.

After about three minutes of just listening and responding in the affirmative, Majesty ends the call.

She says, "That was the lawyer, Arthur. The police didn't have a search warrant, and they didn't read us our rights."

"And?" Arthur interrupts.

She continues, "Attorney Maynard says the police system sucks here in Arizona, and it is crazy how these officers do their jobs halfhearted, and as a result, the court may rule in our favor. He will file a motion to have the charges dismissed."

There is pure celebration in the house. Everyone is relieved and happy. The possibility exists that the charges will be dropped!

Arthur is excited but still on edge. He quickly cautions everyone to remain calm and await the court hearing.

Arthur feels optimistic about the outcome; after all, he hired the best lawyer in Arizona.

On March 17, the long-awaited court date, everyone shows up to court looking their best.

Attorney Maynard looks like he has already won the case, neatly dressed in a well-tailored gray suit.

The courtroom is very intimidating. Majesty, Arthur, Alion, and Labron are seated beside their attorney, while seven police officers are seated to the right. The police officers resemble the arresting officers. The ones who visited the house and arrested Arthur and Labron.

The matter is called up, and the prosecutor says all he needs to say, including how dangerous Arthur and his friends are.

Attorney Maynard gets his chance on the podium. He makes it explicitly clear that the police did not exercise due diligence in doing their job. He also shows evidence that they had no search warrant to go to his client's residence. Neither were they read their rights before being arrested with sufficient supporting documents and statements from Attorney Maynard, the court rules in favor of Arthur and company.

The judge dismisses the cases and tells them they are free to go home.

They thank the attorney and leave the courthouse.

What a relief! They can finally go back to their regular lives, uninterrupted. Or so they think.

Labron and Alion decide to go back to New York.

Majesty still has her friend Stephany in her thoughts and wants to bail her out. She knows Stephany is loyal and could be of help if she has her in the camp. Moreover, she could do with some female company. Arthur agrees as promised, and posts bail for Stephany. They pick her up and take her to a hotel.

Arthur has a way of caring for the people around him. He ensures that everyone is OK. Even Roxanne, there isn't much he can do as she is set for deportation. The most he does is assure her that her family in Jamaica will be taken care of and she will have money when she gets home.

Stephany is elated to be released! Majesty is truly her friend. Majesty gives her some money, a cellphone, new clothes, and a rental car to help her get around and get settled. She promises to get her an attorney to help her with her case. She hires Maynard to represent her. No one except for Kirk ever truly cared for her and treated her with so much respect. The two go out for dinner and speak at length.

Majesty says, "I paid for all your attorney fees; The lawyer will work on your case. He is a great lawyer, and I think you are going to be OK." She continues, "Go see the attorney in the morning and tell him your side of the story. He will take care of everything for you."

Tears stream down her face as she expresses her gratitude.

Majesty whispers, "I got you."

CHAPTER 15
New Beginnings

Arthur and Majesty arrive at the doctor's office. Arthur pushes the door and holds it open for her. Majesty gazes at the room. It has a light blue welcoming color on the wall. A huge poster with the word "Motherhood" written in bold red writing. A picture of two different pregnant women. Another poster. A large picture of a newborn baby is on the opposite side of the wall.

The room is very quiet. Three couples are seated waiting to see the doctor. There is a TV monitor placed on the wall quietly playing a movie.

Arthur walks up to the receptionist. She slides the glass window. To acknowledge their presence, she says, "Good morning. How can I help you? Do you have an appointment?"

Arthur replies, "Yes."

She speaks again. "Please write the name of the patient on this clipboard. Have a seat and wait for your name to be called."

Arthur writes Majesty's name on the clipboard. She gives her a packet to fill out. The receptionist lets him know the cost for the visit will be five hundred dollars. She tells them to have a seat in the lobby. He holds on to Majesty's hand. She leans in as he kisses her on the cheek.

The receptionist calls, "Comala Facey." When they approach the window again, the receptionist asks, "What form of payment will you use for the visit – cash or credit card?"

Arthur replies, "Credit card." He reaches in his pocket, gets his wallet, and makes the payment. He gets his receipt. And they go back to sit.

Soon, a nurse opens the door. She double checks her notepad and shouts, "Comala Facey."

Majesty and Arthur walk over to the nurse. Majesty hands the nurse the packet. She says, "Please come this way." They follow her. She opens Room 4, hands Majesty a gown, and tells her to undress; she will be back. Arthur helps her remove her dress, and she sits on the bed.

When the nurse returns, she puts on a glove and hands Majesty a cup with her name written on it. "Please pee in it," she says. She leads her to the bathroom. Majesty returns and sits on the bed.

In ten minutes, the doctor walks in. "How are you guys doing today? I am Dr. Burrel," he says in a friendly tone.

"We are doing great," answers Arthur.

The doctor washes his hands in the sink and slides on his gloves. He asks, "How long have you been feeling nauseous?"

Majesty answers, "One month."

He examines her stomach and presses gently on her tummy, listens to her heart rate, and takes her vital signs. He stares at the pregnancy test and confirms, "You are pregnant." Majesty feels Arthur looking at her. He is so happy.

Dr. Burrel sets an appointment to see them in a few weeks.

Majesty has mixed emotions. "I wish my mother and father could be here. Arthur, we are expecting our first child," she says, smiling excitedly. He kisses her on her forehead.

He speaks. "Yeah, baby, I wish their grandparents were here with us. Don't worry; I will be the best father in the world. And I know you're going to be a good mother."

She thinks, *Sometimes the dark comes back, the cold blood, it's a part of me, the way I almost killed Alicia in that jail and when I murdered Bob and his followers. I hate to get to that dark place. Can I care for this precious baby?*

They relocate to California to turn a new leaf and begin a fresh start. They have money coming in from different angles, as the marijuana they shipped before the arrest is now paying off. Arthur always thinks of how to expand his borders and generate income. Living lavishly is the only way of life he knows. There is no going back to mediocre, but he vows to be more careful this time.

Majesty is four months pregnant and has a protruding belly. She is overjoyed by how far she has come after losing her parents and is now going to be a parent. She hasn't told Arthur that she is a killer and how she killed six people in one night. "That's something I will keep to myself," she says. "I don't want to scare him off. I must tell Granny Wilma, Merkle, and Miss Mary I am going to be a mommy. Arthur is over the moon. It will be his first son, and he must set things up so his son won't ever have to do the illegal stuff. He has to have a great life."

All is not bright in their world; it is approaching the end of the six months that immigration allowed Majesty to be in the country. In just one week, she will become an undocumented immigrant. The only way to change her fate is if she gets married to a U.S. citizen.

Arthur will not let her leave; she is everything to him. They are in sync with how they breathe, think, and smell each other; he doesn't have to say a word, and she knows what he is saying. They went to jail together. She understood the assignment; she could've gotten scared and told the police everything, but she held it like a G. He has crazy respect for her, and he doesn't even want to know another woman, so he proposes. She is the love of his life, and she is carrying his baby! He wants to spend the rest of his life with her.

* * *

She has little time to plan her wedding. The thought of getting everyone together makes her excited. She hasn't seen her family in so long. The process of getting them together makes her exhausted. Her partner is wealthy, so he hires a professional wedding planner to take the pressure off.

Majesty's family is excited to hear of her marriage to Arthur. They know of him and know how he treats her. Her grandparents, Miss Mary, and her aunts will be present.

She makes the decision to have both grandfathers, Septemus and Kester, walk her down the aisle. She hasn't asked them yet! It is a surprise.

The wedding date is drawing closer, and the plans are being finalized. They decide to get married in Florida at the Palm Hotel and Spa.

They fly their family and friends in and arrange accommodations for everyone to stay at the same hotel.

The day of the wedding is finally here. Arthur's parents and siblings are in attendance. A few of his old friends are also present. The wedding is in the grandest ballroom the hotel has available. The color scheme is ivory and burgundy. It is regal. The perfectly orchestrated band recites soothing music while guests gracefully find their seats.

The aisle is lined with a white runner strategically placed for the bride to make her grand entrance. The aroma of the natural gourmet cuisine can be detected from miles away. It is the perfect setting. Majesty is busy getting ready in the presidential suite. She has her family and friends with her. Stephany is her maid of honor. The ceremony is to be held in the ballroom, and the reception is to be hosted on the beach.

"The indoor-outdoor wedding is an excellent choice," says Majesty. The location is perfect. The building is immaculate. Guests were previously informed that the reception is on the beach, so they need to be prepared to take their shoes off.

It is a traditional wedding. Majesty asks both Septemus and Kester to walk her down the aisle, and they are both ecstatic to do so. Arthur is now in position waiting on his bride. His groomsmen are standing behind him, providing intermittent comfort as needed.

It is the moment everyone has anticipated. Here comes the bride.

Septemus and Kester, on either side, walk their granddaughter down the aisle and hand her off to Arthur.

She is the most beautiful bride anyone has ever seen. She wears a white dress, strapless with lace and diamond details on the upper corset. The lower half is flowing, hiding her baby bump. She looks angelic.

The wedding ceremony lasts for approximately 45 minutes. The diamond ring he places on her left-hand shimmers from a distance. The master of ceremonies announces that it is time to take their shoes off and head to the beach for the rest of the night.

The reception is beautiful; the food is spectacular. As it gets darker, the sunset creates a romantic ambiance.

Majesty gets tired. She concludes her night and goes back to the suite with her husband.

She knows she has little time with her family, so they postpone their honeymoon by a day to have a little family gathering the following day.

The next morning, both families meet for breakfast. Getting to know each other and catching up on good times is lovely.

They spend the day together, and everyone says their goodbyes in the afternoon. Majesty is elated. The series of events over the past couple of months has been very overwhelming. From getting locked up to being freed, to being pregnant and now a married woman! Life really has a way of surprising you.

Arthur plans a romantic getaway for the honeymoon. He doesn't plan a long getaway as they must return to work shortly.

They ride a very fancy yacht to Atlantic Keys. It offers romance and beautiful views. The feel of the Caribbean breeze, the dolphins, and the colorful coral reef is a sight to behold. They check into a luxury hotel on the coast. It is an ideal location for a night of fun. They enjoy each other's company, Mr. and Ms. Bitting!

The honeymoon is short-lived, but for a good reason. The two have a grand idea while in the Atlantic Keys. They need to find a way to take over the west coast. Majesty is now a green card holder and no longer needs to live in fear. She is a mother! She has a bouncing baby boy. He resembles his father. His name is Demetre Bitting.

The newlywed parents purchase a lovely family home in Beverly

Hills. It is a two-story modern house consisting of five bedrooms with a bathroom for each room, a family room, a large kitchen, a dining room, and an office for them to conduct business.

The home is decorated to suit her needs. It sports a pool beneath the couple's bedroom. Majesty loves it!

With operating a large business, they need people to keep the house and take care of their son, Demetre. So, they have a full-time nanny, Ms. B.; a housekeeper, Mrs. Sharp; and a chef, Itory. They also have a few drivers on call as needed.

Majesty and her husband are very wise entrepreneurs. Based on experience, they know it is best not to keep all their income in one place. They have to find different areas to invest in.

Later that year, they open a boutique on Rodeo Drive, selling high-end fashion items. Soon, it becomes a hotspot for people in the area. Business is booming. She has Miss Mary rent out her parent's house. She now lives in the States.

The marijuana business is still in operation. They rent a warehouse in Los Angeles, where they can comfortably operate from. They get houses in the area for Stephany, Labron, and Alion and vehicles of their choice. Things are falling into place; they have a loyal team around them who will ensure they are always protected, and the business is done according to plan. Everyone must always check their rearview mirror not to be followed.

Stephany becomes the newest family member of the gang after she is released from jail. All her charges were dropped, and she decides to roll with Majesty. She knows she got a new lease on life and is grateful.

Alion and Labron are always with Arthur. They are his trusted and loyal soldiers.

From the first day Stephany sees Labron, she blushes. She thinks he is cute; she keeps it to herself.

Every Monday, a large shipment of marijuana is delivered to the warehouse in Los Angeles. The team ensures it's repacked and distributed to the respective locations. Operations are smooth, consistent, and discreet.

CHAPTER 16

Hit

Cocaine and heroin are in high demand from the customers, and after a long discussion, they decide they will venture into the field. They know the risks, and know the penal punishment is greater, but they also know the benefits, and it is a risk worth taking.

They are moving up in the game, gaining respect, and creating enemies.

They decide to open a nightclub and call it Club Vegas. It is the perfect place to turn the drug money over and to conduct business discreetly. Everything is running smoothly. It is the new spot for locals and tourists.

Stephany is at the top of the list every weekend; it is easy for her to monitor the business in the club as she is a natural party animal, so she fits in perfectly.

All the beautiful women come out to gyrate their bodies and have a good time. The men came to flirt and meet the finest of the finest to take home.

One Friday night, while having fun, Stephany bumps into a gentleman. He looks vaguely familiar, but his facial features have changed, so she isn't quite sure who he is. After a brief conversation and exchange of pleasantries, she realizes it is Kirk, her long-lost friend.

"Oh shit, Kirk!" she exclaims, "What the heck are you doing here?" She continues, "I haven't seen you in years!"

Kirk is the only person who knows that she murdered her uncle. He is the one who got rid of the weapon and covered for her. He helped her escape and told everyone someone else killed him.

"Stef, this is unreal, of all the places, the club. But then again, it's you, so yes, it's real," laughs Kirk.

She laughs and slaps him on his shoulder. She says in disbelief, "Kirk, how are you?"

"I have been doing great, sis! I missed you," he replies with a grin. "I know I can talk to you about anything. After you left, I got caught up in the Faceoff Crew. I regret doing it, but I am here now, and I guess I am stuck. Badaz is the leader. He is a shitbag. I hate him!"

Stephany is intrigued. She knows the Faceoff Crew is the initial crew of LA, and word on the street is that they are now threatened by her bosses, Majesty and Arthur.

He continues, "Steph, I've always thought about you and hoped you were OK. Look at you now, so grown and sexy."

In a concerned tone, she asks, "So, isn't Badaz a good person? I heard he owns Asylum Night Club."

He replies, "Good person? He is a pussy. He doesn't believe anyone else should eat in life! He doesn't give his gang members opportunities. I don't even own a car; I have to borrow his car, and I can use it only if it's available. He only treats his right-hand men Adisha and Binns with respect. The rest of the crew can go to hell."

"Even this club, Stef. He is upset with the owners of this club for taking away all his patrons because this is the new hot spot. Badaz is upset because this club is taking over the West Coast. He believes he runs this turf." At this point, Stephany has all her antennas up.

He laments, "I really love you, so if you don't need to be here next Friday, please stay away because they are planning to shoot up this club. They sent me out here to check it out."

Stephany is shocked and angry at the same time. She says, "This is my place; my bosses run this club. How dare anyone even think of destroying their livelihood?" She is eager to get in touch with her bosses.

They have to figure out a way to stop this hit!

She promises Kirk she will stay away. They make plans to meet for drinks another time, after which they say their goodbyes and go their separate ways.

CHAPTER 17

The Meeting

Badaz Brooks is a slender five-foot-eight-inch man, born in Crenshaw, California. His mother was a stay-at-home mom, while his father ran a large drug-for-guns trade ring. The nature of this lifestyle is very risky and, at times, leads to either death or jail. His father was murdered when he was only 10 years old. He witnessed this, and not long after, his mother was murdered by her gangster drug dealer boyfriend. He went from foster home to foster home. He was dealt a raw hand in life and decided from an early age he wanted to be like his father.

At the age of 19, he became a drug lord and crime boss like his father. From his father's legacy, he gained the respect of many people in Crenshaw, so it wasn't hard for him to be in charge. He controlled the West Coast and had a sizable network of people working for him in the illegal drugs for gun trade. Badaz is the leader of the Faceoff Crew in Crenshaw; he owns and operates the Asylum Night Club.

It was the hottest thing in LA until the opening of Club Vegas, owned and operated by Arthur and Majesty.

Badaz has his gang of faithful soldiers, Kirk included. Kirk is Stephany's childhood friend. His right-hand man is a tall, slender

Caucasian man, entirely covered in tattoos. His name is Anthony White III, aka Adisha.

Adisha is a very loyal friend. He spent ten years in prison for a murder that Badaz had committed. They become inseparable. Badaz takes good care of his family and ensures all his needs are met daily.

To date, Adisha is still his most faithful friend. He willingly takes care of any business without second-guessing the repercussions. Badaz learns of the new hot club in the area and is threatened. He knows sales are declining in his establishment, and so is the crowd. He considers it a big disrespect and knows he has to put a stop to it. Badaz calls a meeting with his team. "Adisha, we must do something about this. I need a meeting with the owners of Club Vegas. Clearly, they are unaware of who the real boss is. They can have their little club, but I must receive a percentage of what they make, after all, this is my territory. Arrange a meeting for Monday."

As usual, Adisha is on top of it. The meeting is set up.

Stephany immediately tells Majesty and the crew that she ran into Kirk, her childhood friend. She says he is part of Badaz's gang and tells them about the hit the crew has on their club. She knows it is serious business.

Stephany, Alion, and Labron are at the gun range, which they do regularly. They enjoy sharpening their shooting skills and betting on who will win the sharpshooter competition of the day. Stephany feels the vibration from her cellphone that is in her back pocket. She pauses for a second to take the call. It is her boss. She answers, "Hello, boss, what's going on?" She spends three minutes just nodding and responding in the affirmative. After ending the call, she says to the others, "Yow, that was the boss lady. She needs to see us right away."

The trio pulls up to the headquarters where the bosses are situated.

Without hesitation, Majesty starts the meeting. "Today, Arthur got a very strange phone call with no caller ID. The person on the other end of the line informed him that the leader of the Faceoff Crew would love to meet with him to discuss future plans at the Asylum Night Club and to set some things straight," she continues. "The person went further to state that we are treading on very dangerous waters, and we need to watch our backs."

Alion laughs in an evil tone and says, "Sounds like a threat to me, and we don't take threats lightly."

Labron chimes in, "Got that right, but if they want war, we have the infantry, so tell us what to do, boss."

Arthur interrupts, "Relax, guys, it's just a meeting, but we must prepare for the worst because these niggas can't be trusted."

Majesty and Stephany are in a reflective mood, trying to figure out their next move. Stephany suggests, "I think we should all be armed and ready in case anyone tries to sideline us."

"Good idea," says Majesty. "Be safe, guys. We will reconvene on Monday at 10 a.m. to go meet with Badaz."

They adjourn the meeting and go about their ways. On Monday, as discussed, the team meets at the warehouse and gets aboard two separate black Suburbans. They head to the Asylum Night Club. Stephany, Alion, and Labron stay in the car as Majesty and Arthur go inside to meet with Badaz. Even though it is midday, the interior of the club is dark. It isn't during hours of operation and so it is quiet. Two men are seen dressed in all black standing at either entrance as if they are guarding the establishment.

Unbothered, Arthur and Majesty make their way to the back of the club where the office is located. They are met by Adisha, who escorts them into Badaz's office. He sits at a large wooden desk covered with cigars and exotic whiskeys. He has a lit cigar in his mouth. "Sit," he beckons to them. The couple obliges. Majesty scrutinizes the office for the poor décor and foul smell. She spots a deer head pinned to the wall and a bull's eye target. Badaz extends his hand for a shake. "Bitting, is it?"

Arthur politely declines and says, "No time for pleasantries, respectfully. What is the purpose of this meeting?"

Badaz laughs, "Club Vegas is now starting to become a problem to my business. You can keep your club, but this is my turf. You are fucking with my money, and I don't like that. So, here's the deal, I need half of everything you make, and that is non-negotiable. If not, things will start to get ugly for you and your wife."

Arthur asks, "Is that a threat, Mr. Badaz?"

Badaz responds, "Call it what you may."

Arthur replies, "I am not sure I can do that. I have people to feed."

"OK, well, if you don't have my money by Friday, then I have no choice but to get it by force. You are dismissed."

Majesty isn't satisfied that she didn't get a word in, so she chimes in, "Badaz, are you trying to extort us? We are all here to eat. What you are saying is ridiculous. There is no way we can give you half of everything. We can close the club on Wednesdays, one of our busiest nights, and you open that night, and we all be happy."

He replies, "No, I want half of everything."

She says, "OK, since you don't want to come to an amicable decision, I guess it is what it is then. You are walking on a very thin line. You can do what you want, but I am a Jamaican woman, and if you fuck with my family and my livelihood, you fuck with me, and if you fuck with me, that's a whole different can of worms." The dark and cold-blooded side pops out.

Arthur glimpses over to his wife, surprised. He thinks *Majesty is brave. She has not an ounce of fear in her tone.*

"Is that a threat, young lady?" Badaz asks in a concerned tone.

"It's Mrs. Bitting to you, and no, it's not a threat. It's a promise."

They leave the office angry and ready for war.

The two vehicles return to the warehouse, where they convene again. "That asshole wants to extort us. He is asking for 50 percent of everything we earn," Majesty laments.

Alion is livid. "He must be drunk. He is not getting a red cent of your hard-earned money, boss."

Labron agrees. "Exactly, just say the word, one phone call, and his three points will be taken."

Arthur is pacing back and forth. He is angry. He works hard for his family and to be where he is today. How could this man try to take it away? He is adamant that he isn't paying a dollar to Badaz. The next few days, the crew spends every day preparing for the planned attack.

Friday is the payout day, and no money is sent to Badaz. He is furious. He knows what he has to do. That same afternoon, he instructs his gang to attack the Vegas nightclub.

His aim is to murder the owner. He fails miserably. The Bittings know of his plans, so they spend as little time at the club as they can.

The Faceoff Crew killed six innocent people. Though involved in criminal activities, Arthur is a man for the people. He is very caring and hates to see people hurt. He is furious about the death of his patrons, and he tells his wife justice must be served for those innocent people. He must send a message and let them know who the real boss is.

Majesty's mind flickers to her dark, cold, and bloody past. *This Badaz guy is getting me upset. I cannot control my temper; my anxiety is getting the best of me.* She paces back and forth.

Months later, Arthur and Majesty pay a settlement to the deceased families.

They refurbish the club with a facelift and reopen Club Vegas. Business is booming again.

Stephany speaks to Kirk after the attack and gets him to divulge the area that Badaz frequents. She has a plan. Badaz enjoys spending money on girls, especially curvy Hawaiians. Stephany fits the description.

She does everything in her womanly power to catch his attention. Stephany visits Badaz's nightclub every so often and ensures she makes herself seen. She always dresses the way he likes and makes eye contact with him. She is irresistible, and not long after, he falls for it. The two are "dating." Stephany spends a lot of time with him and gets him to trust her. One night, she tells him she needs privacy with him, so he needs to get rid of his bodyguards.

At first, he is apprehensive, but her tight satin dress with thigh-high splits and low-cut neckline cloud his judgment, and he obliges. Stephany seduces him and shows him a good time. While he is distracted by her legs on his chest, she drugs his drink.

Three hours later, the great Badaz wakes up in a warehouse surrounded by Arthur, Majesty, Stephany, Alion, and Labron. To his left, he sees some tools, knives, a wrench, chains, matchsticks, gasoline, ice pick, and other unimaginable torture devices.

"You fucking bitch," Badaz exclaims, while wrestling to get out of the bondage he is in. His hand is tied up behind the chair he is sitting in, with his feet bound.

Majesty slaps him across the face. She remembers her training from Miss Mary. "How dare you call her a bitch?"

"I am going to kill you!" he screams.

"Not if we kill you first," Stephany responds.

He sees Arthur, and right away, he realizes he is in trouble. "We meet again! This time on my turf."

Arthur signals to Alion. Alion punches Badaz as hard as he can. Blood gushes, and a tooth flies out of his mouth. Badaz doesn't say a word; he just spits the blood from his mouth. Arthur continues, "You shot up my establishment, killing innocent people. How dare you? You are a weak, washed-up don! How do you suppose we punish you for wreaking such havoc in our lives?"

Badaz laments, "You will never get away with this. Adisha and the others will be searching for me, and they will find me."

Labron says, "How? Remember you dismissed them last night for some pussy you thought you would get, so no one will look for you. Tomorrow, maybe, but by then, you will be long gone."

Majesty steps up to him. "I told you, I am a Jamaican woman." She spits a few indecent words. "Jamaican woman scorn."

They torture him. They pull his fingernails out, demanding that he give them the code for his safe. They cut pieces of his skin off, until he tells them where to find the list of suppliers and buyers he does business with. Too much to bear, he sings like a bird. He tells them about all his connections and where they can find all his money. He is, at this point, begging to live.

When they have no use for him and have all the information they need, Alion murders him execution-style. Then, he cuts off his head, packs it neatly in a box, and has it hand-delivered to the Asylum Night Club. They know once his crew finds Badaz's head, war will be declared, and it will be messy for the next couple of days. So, they decide to work behind the scenes, making connections and lying low.

CHAPTER 18
Paradise

With all the drama that unfolded, the team decides it is time for a vacation. In addition, Demetre has never met his maternal family, and the rest of the gang is excited to visit Jamaica. They decide to plan a vacation to the beautiful island and birthplace of Majesty and Arthur.

It is exciting and the trip worth looking forward to; however, they have to make a business stop first. They take the private jet and go to Venice to meet with Romeo, one of Badaz's previous clients. They meet in an upscale restaurant. Romeo explains that his source from Lost Angeles had been murdered a few weeks ago in the most gruesome way. He was beheaded.

Majesty is so sympathetic; she extends her sympathies and condemns the act even though he is the contact they tortured out of Badaz. In the same breath, Arthur reassures him that they will ensure his business will be handled professionally and promptly. Romeo wants quality products; Arthur knows he can provide this and then some! He reassures him they can send one container of product a month, and once he is pleased, they will increase his shipment. Romeo is pleased with the proposal. They shake hands and end the meeting, creating a new business relationship. The team is now ready to relax, unwind, and get their suntans on!

* * *

"Welcome to the beautiful island of Jamaica, where the temperature is just right. Thank you for flying with us, and enjoy your stay."

Stephany is living her dream. Dressed for the weather, she is wearing shorts and a crop top in tropical prints. A pair of sandals and a broad straw hat. Alion and Labron are ready for some Caribbean girls. "Where are the Jamaican hotties?"

Majesty and Arthur are excited to be home with Demetre. They are reminiscing; this is where it all began! The couple has a surprise for Alion. They are greeted by a gentleman in a three-piece tuxedo holding their names on a whiteboard. He escorts the group to their transportation, a seven-seater Tahoe truck, which Arthur had pre-rented. When they enter the truck, Roxanne is in the back, smiling. Alion is so excited to see his girlfriend. They introduce her to Stephany. Roxanne was deported back to Jamaica after they were all arrested in Phoenix. Arthur has continued to assist her with caring for her family and has her take care of the Jamaican portion of their business. She hands Arthur the bag of guns he requested; he knows he is on business and the crew must stay strapped.

Roxanne couples up with her man, Alion, kissing and chatting softly. Stephany shouts, "Get a room!" Everyone is laughing. Stephany is eyeing Labron. He looks away from her as though he is doing something wrong.

When they arrive at the hotel where they had made reservations, Majesty collects the keys from the receptionist and hands them to every-one. They all take their belongings to their rooms. Majesty is happy to be back home; she tells the nanny to take Demetre, and she will get him in a few. She needs to get some sleep. She kisses her son and follows behind her husband to their room. After an hour of resting, she relieves the nanny from her duties. They decide to go for a swim in the hotel pool. Arthur puts Demetre on his shoulder, trying to teach him to swim.

Majesty loves the water. She splashes the water onto Arthur's face and plays with their son, who is laughing uncontrollably as his dad spins him in the pool. They have so much fun. She tells him she wants to visit her grandparents and Miss Mary later that evening. When they return to their room, Demetre is running away from his mom. She has to chase him in the lobby to catch him. After dinner, he is sound asleep. They put him in his bed. Arthur and she drive out and head to Waterford.

On their way, she says, "Arthur, I need to tell you something, and I don't want to keep any secrets from you. I told you that my parents got murdered when I was eight years old.

"Well, I witnessed the murder. A drug dealer named Bob and two of his friends killed my parents execution-style and burned my house down. Bob and his friends showed up at my parent's funeral pretending to care. The funny thing is he didn't know I saw the whole thing. I kept it to myself. I took revenge when I turned eighteen years old, on my parent's anniversary. I killed six people that night, Bob's friends, including his sick mother and sister. They took a part of me. I couldn't let my parents die in vain. I didn't want to tell you because I was afraid I would chase you away."

Arthur is so surprised he says, "Baby, don't sweat it. This is the world we live in today. People can bring the worst out of you sometimes. I don't love you any less. I would have done the same thing."

They drive across Crossway Bridge into Waterford. When they arrive, she goes to Miss Mary's house. She rings her doorbell. When she sees her, Miss Mary hugs her; she hugs Arthur and welcomes them inside her home. She tells her the tenant who rented her parent's house is very nice. They catch up on Demetre and the plans for their trip. Majesty gives Miss Mary some cash to help her out with expenses. They look at her parent's house and leave shortly. They visit Wilma and Merkle, leaving them money too. They all eat dinner and go back to the hotel.

The following morning, they visit Dunn's River Falls. After making a few calls to her friends and family, she lies beside her husband and gives him a massage; he loves it when his wife pampers him. She goes for the baby oil and starts to oil down his body. He starts kissing her uncontrollably; they make sweet love and go to bed butt-naked. In the morning, Majesty gets the breakfast order from everyone and then calls for room service. After breakfast, they all get dressed and head to Dunn's River Fall.

On their way to Dunn's River Falls, Stephany looks through the vehicle window and sees children playing along the side of the road. Stray dogs, old people, and food/fruit stalls are everywhere.

This is paradise, she thinks to herself. *This is what Majesty was telling me about this beautiful island when we were in jail. It's like a breath of fresh air.*

When they arrive, Arthur pays the entrance fee for everyone. Security opens the gates, and they drive in and find a parking spot. They need climbing shoes. There is a haberdashery opposite the entrance, which sells memorabilia and everything you need for the climb and the water.

They buy shoes to help them navigate the climb safely. The rocks are sharp, and you can wound your foot if you're not careful.

When he returns to the vehicle, Majesty and Ms. B. follow behind Arthur. He carries his son on his neck. Alion, Stephany, Roxanne, and Labron are not too far behind them. Many tourists are waiting in line to go to the top of the falls. They join the back of the line, following a lady in an orange bathing suit with her family. Everyone is having fun, laughing, meeting and greeting. The tour guys help everyone to go up safely. The natural air is crisp, the green trees blowing a fresh breeze.

Dunn's River Falls is one of Jamaica's most famous attractions. It is beautiful. The cascading waterfall that empties into the sea. The gorgeous white-sand beach with gentle shallow water, is perfect for swimming. Tourists from all walks of life want to experience the majestic display. The farther you climb, the more beautiful the view. After climbing the rocks, a path takes them to crystal-clear seawater. It is amazing; they are all feeling total bliss. It is good to see everyone is experiencing this beautiful place.

Majesty and Arthur get to spend some quality time together. They make love on the island every chance they get. Later that night, they sit on their balcony, smoking a blunt and planning to take over the world. This is truly what they needed to reset, refocus, readjust, and restart.

The following morning, Roxanne directs them to Westmoreland, making a right turn and taking them off the main road. It is a lonely dirt track with bushes on either side. No life is seen within a three-mile radius. After ten minutes of traveling on the dirt track, they come to a stop in front of a small board structure. They all follow behind Roxanne and Arthur. They can smell the fresh aroma of cultivated marijuana. Three towering men with dreadlocks emerge from the wooden shed, holding M16 rifles.

Tafari, the boss who awaits them, is dressed in a multicolored vest, khaki pants, and nude Desert Clarks, his hair wrapped in a red turban. He says, "Hey, Roxanne, how are you?"

She replies, "Hello, Tafari, this is Arthur and Majesty, my bosses."

Arthur says, "Hey Tafari, how are you? I can smell how strong the marijuana is."

Tafari replies, "You are at the right place if it is a strong herb you want."

They all laugh. He leads them to the back of the building, where he has acres of marijuana. He asks, "What grade are you looking for?"

Arthur answers, "The highest grade, organic, dried, and cured in the best condition. I need one container sealed and ready to import to Italy in one week."

Tafari replies, "Yes, I have my connection at the wharf. I can get the container and have it shipped out to Italy. To pack, deliver, and use my connection at the wharf is eighty-thousand dollars."

Majesty hands the money to Roxanne, who hands it over to Tafari. They walk back to their truck and leave with the understanding that business is set and should be ready within the next week.

The crew gets back in the truck and goes to visit their families. They stop and buy jerk ackee and saltfish chicken, jerk pork, and festival with mannish water soup and chicken soup. Stephany is impressed with the seasoning. The food is so delicious.

For the first time in her life, she feels like she belongs to a family. She feels loved and appreciated; no one is trying to sleep with her, just real, true love. The unit is like a family. She enjoys every moment of it.

Alion and Roxanne visit his grandparents and leave them money; Labron does the same with his family. Majesty and Arthur take Demetre to visit their grandparents on both sides. He is all over the place, enjoying every attention from his cousins, aunties, Miss Mary, Merkle, and Wilma. They are happy to see their great-grandson. Merkle says, "I wish Winnie and Dehon could see how beautiful you are, Majesty, and your beautiful family."

Wilma says, "They are watching over her and protecting her." Tears fill Majesty's eyes as she remembers her loving parents.

When they get back to the hotel, they are all so exhausted they shower and go to bed. Ms. B. loves taking care of Demetre; she would do anything for her bosses, Arthur and Majesty. They believed in her when she had nothing; they bought her a home in LA and sent her grandson to college tuition-free. They give her an opportunity; she is loyal, trustworthy. The Bittings love and respect her; she is like a mother to them. She takes care of their son like her own child. She loves Demetre. Ms. B sees money lying around all the time in the Bittings' home, and she never takes a penny; she is well-paid and is very grateful.

CHAPTER 19

Pay Up!

Waking up to the sound of the ocean birds chirping and the warm sun is like a dream come true. Doing it next to the love of her life is paradise. As she rolls over and kisses him, she says, "Baby, I know this is nice, but we got to get up."

Arthur hugs his wife and kisses her on her forehead. He groans, "Do we really?" and covers his face with the pillow.

She jumps on top of him and says, "Did we get rich by sleeping? Come on, lazy butt, it's time to grind."

He slaps her on her posterior and rolls out of bed. "OK, boss." They both grin. "Baby, I want to check with Tafari to see how things are progressing." Majesty agrees.

She then wakes her son up. The three play around in the room for a while before Majesty gets him dressed for breakfast. After breakfast, Majesty tells Ms. B. she will go and do some business so she can hang out with Demetre at the hotel; it has a lot of amenities.

They have a business to conduct and don't want the baby to be around. They will meet up with them later. They all jump in the truck and head for Westmoreland to see Tafari. When they arrive, Tafari comes out of the shed. He looks as if he was attacked by a pack of wolves. His eyes are black and blue, his lips are swollen, and dried old blood can be seen on his face. His left hand is in a bandage, as if it is broken, and the old shirt was used to save it from falling off.

His face looks as if he sees a ghost. Before Arthur gets the chance to ask what happened, Tafari says, "Arthur, this man from Buff Road named Whimpy, he was not happy I was doing business with you. He beat me and took all your money. I can still do the container of weed, but I am going to need some help with the shipping, and he warned me that if I ever open my mouth, he will remove my tongue and cut me into small pieces," a clearly shaken Tafari shares.

"Who is he, and where does he live?"

Tafari is now worried. He knows how dangerous the top man can be. "Bossy, just leave this alone. I will still give you the weed, but this man is dangerous. He will kill you and come back and kill me and my family."

Arthur isn't fazed; after all, he has just taken down the most powerful man in Los Angeles, so he knows this "top man" will be a walk in the park. Plus, he knows he has his team behind him. He says in a stern voice, "TAKE ME TO HIM."

Tafari is now confused but obliges. It's almost as if he had to choose the better of the two evils. If he doesn't take him to the top man, Arthur will probably hurt him, and if he does, the top man is going to kill him. Poor Tafari.

He gets in the truck and directs them toward the man's house.

"You can stay in the vehicle. You don't have to come out," says Arthur. As they pull closer to the man's house, four men are seen playing dominoes in the front of the yard. Obviously frightened, Tafari lets some indecent language spill out of his mouth and says, "He is wearing the gray shirt."

Majesty asks Tafari, "What is his name?"

He answers, "Whimpy." Everyone takes out their guns and exits the vehicle except Tafari and Roxanne. They stay in the vehicle.

Tafari shakes his head and says to himself, "This is going to end badly."

Arthur approaches the men. They immediately stop playing while trying to retrieve their guns. But Alion is quicker. He pulls his Glock and says, "Nobody moves, nobody gets hurt. Hold your hands up in the air."

The men are shocked. Labron has his gun pointed at the men and orders them to walk around the dominoes table until otherwise instructed. They each ambush a person. Arthur has Whimpy at gunpoint. He uses his Uzi submachine gun to slap Whimpy across his face. Blood gushes from his face. The rest of his crew sit around the table looking helpless, with their hands in the air.

Arthur asks, "Whimpy are you a bank?"

Whimpy looks puzzled.

Arthur says, "You collect people's money, and I think you have something for me."

Whimpy answers, "I don't even know you. What are you talking about?"

Majesty says, "You have my money. The money you took from Tafari." At this point, both Majesty and Arthur are irritated and just need their money back.

"Oh, is your money?" he answers in a quiet voice. He is trying to get up. Arthur pushes him back into the chair.

"The money is inside," he stutters. He says, "Biggs knows where it is. He can go get it."

He points to the fat man at the table. Stephany has her gun on the fat man. She uses the gun and directs him inside. Shortly after, they emerge with a bag of money. Stephany shoots the man with the money in his head and takes the bag from him, and steps over him. When Whimpy sees this, he pees his pants.

Whimpy says in a frightened voice, "Boss, I didn't know it was your money."

Arthur says, "Now you know. If Tafari tells me, you fuck with him again. A few pieces of indecent language leave his mouth. This time, you will shit your pants."

They jump in the car and speed off. Tafari is nervous but happy to see Whimpy humbled. When they get back to Tafari's place, he thanks them for what they did. Majesty jokes, "I bet he won't come around again."

They count the money and realize it is $50,000 over the amount they paid Tafari. Tafari is now feeling large and in charge. He calls Whimpy's cellphone and says, "Pussy, you gave us extra, come get your blood money."

Whimpy wants nothing to do with Tafari after his encounter with the Bittings. In a shaky voice, he says, "Keep it."

Tafari says, "Oh, you quiet now, don't come back over my yard, pussy."

Majesty tells Tafari to keep the extra $50,000. "Just make sure we get back on schedule." Tafari has so much respect for these people. He wants everything to go perfectly.

He leads them to a private shed in the back and shows them the strongest grade he has. He says for what they did for him, he will give them a gift with no additional charge. He salutes them, and they drive off. A few days later, Arthur calls Tafari to check on the status of his shipment. This time, everything is good to go. And the container is ready for shipment. Arthur makes several calls to his connections at the various ports.

Arthur calls Romeo to inform him that the shipment is on its way and he should expect a call on the day of arrival. Romeo is impressed. "Let's hope this is quality weed I am getting." He continues, "If this shipment goes through Arthur, I will order two containers from you."

"Romeo gave us a time, and everything is on the right schedule," says Arthur

Majesty nods.

Everything is going according to plan. It is time to get back to reality. It is time to go home. He tells the crew that things might get crazy now that they are going back after they murdered Badaz. He tells them, "Brace yourself and be careful!"

CHAPTER 20
Back to Reality

They arrive at LAX International Airport. Everyone is missing Jamaica. Alion is thinking about Roxanne and wondering how she could move back here without Immigration bothering her. Maybe he can have her come by boat. He really cares about her, and her living in Jamaica is very difficult for both of them. They talk on the phone every day, but this long-distance relationship is getting to him.

Stephany gets in her truck and heads home. She has brought back lots of seasoning and trinkets for memories. She thinks to herself as she hits the highway, *I would live in Jamaica. It was so peaceful, even though I had to kill that man to set an example for Whimpy. I bet he will never mess with anyone anymore.*

Labron is happy to take a break from the hustle and bustle. He feels rejuvenated. The trip cleared his mind, and he is ready to return to work as he speeds off. When he gets to his apartment, he has been thinking about Stephany on a different level. He thinks to himself, *Maybe I should invite her to dinner one day. Nah, she is like a sister to me. It's money over bitches. I am not ready to settle down yet. I cannot see myself with one girl for the rest of my life. I have to have them in a different race, different culture.* He smiles and shakes his head.

CHAPTER 21

Broken Heart

They say home is where the heart is. The team finally arrives safely in California. Arthur is an active father; he enjoys doing things with his son. He ensures he makes the time to do the things his son likes. One afternoon, while playing with Demetre, he falls to the floor.

Demetre is jumping on him and laughing. "Daddy, get up!" But Arthur is not responding.

Majesty thinks it's a joke, so she ignores them. She realizes he has been down for a while and showing no signs of awareness. That is when she goes to her husband and says, "Baby, that's enough. You are scaring me. Get up."

Majesty notices he isn't breathing, and instantly, she feels a lump in her throat. She screams for help, and Ms. B. and the housekeeper come running. "Call 911, Arthur isn't breathing." Demetre starts crying, so the nanny takes him to his room. The housekeeper dials 911 and hands the phone to Majesty.

She is calling his name. "Arthur, Arthur!" No response. Majesty is crying while answering the questions of the operator. She is instructed to remain calm and follow the instructions given to help save her husband's life. She agrees. She gives him mouth-to-mouth resuscitation.

Majesty does it a few times, and nothing changes. She is then told to do chest compressions. As she follows the directions of the operator, she is reassured that the ambulance is on its way.

Majesty can hear the siren from a distance; she can't wait for them to arrive to bring help because she knows she isn't doing it correctly. Majesty makes way for the EMTs to save her husband. There are three uniformed personnel. One asks for basic information for registration purposes, while the other two work assiduously on Arthur. They cut open his shirt and attach the external defibrillator. They deliver an electric shock trying to restore a normal heart rhythm. While two EMTs work on him, the other EMT asks, "What is his name and birth date? Can you tell me what happened?"

"His name is Arthur Bitting, and his date of birth is October 23," she tells him as she points to where she has been standing. "I was in the Florida room while he was playing with our son, then I heard when he fell on the floor. I thought he was playing around, and then I noticed he wasn't moving or breathing. That's when I called you guys." She relays the details as best she can.

"Is he allergic to any medication? Does he have any sickness we should know about?" the specialist asks.

She wipes the tears and softly answers, "Nothing that I know of." As she watches them work on him, she feels helpless and nervous.

"We got a pulse. Let's get him in right now," says another EMT.

Majesty sighs in relief. She shouts, "YES! Thank you, God!"

They call it in, put him on a stretcher, and wheel him into the ambulance. Majesty puts on her shoes, and the housekeeper hands her her pocketbook. She jumps in the ambulance with him, and they speed off. She holds on to his limp hand and starts crying. She prays and asks God to breathe life into her husband. She prays for the strength to deal with whatever is coming. She tells God that if her husband survives, she will start serving him.

When they arrive at the Emergency Room, they rush him in with doctors and nurses surrounding him. It is a blur. Pure chaos. Majesty is told she has to wait in the lobby. She paces back and forth, biting her nails. She is worried for her husband. She can't begin to imagine what to do if something were to happen to him. She opens her pocketbook, grabs her phone, and calls Stephany. She tells her to come to the hospital and come alone. She sits in the waiting room lounge, obviously exhausted and heartbroken. Each time a doctor exits the ER, she stands up, hoping it is news about her husband. Each time, she is disappointed it isn't.

She reminisces about the memories they had together. From the day she met her husband in Jamaica, him marrying her, her going to jail, having their son, all the trips they took, buying their first house together, all the sacrifices they made as a team, and everything else they did as a couple. She smiles to herself. The more she thinks of losing him, the more she panics and can't help but cry. As she is about to get up and start pacing again, she sees Stephany rushing through the building's main entrance.

She hugs her tight. She just needs someone. She needs a friend. Stephany asks, "What happened?" Majesty tells her while shaking her head. Stephany comforts her, and they sit and wait for about an hour, after which a doctor comes out.

"Ms. Bitting?" he asks in an African accent.

Majesty jumps to her feet, "That's me, I'm Ms. Bitting. How is my husband?"

"I am Doctor Ogobuwu." Majesty holds on to Stephany's hand. Her heart is racing, and her palms are sweating. "Your husband suffered a heart attack; luckily, you got help when you did. We operated and put a pacemaker in."

The doctor continues, "He must take better care of himself. The pacemaker will extend his life, but he must do his part. A heart attack is no joke. Tell your husband to slow down."

"Can we see him?" asks Stephany.

"Yes! He is resting. Follow me." He leads them to Arthur's room. When they arrive, he is still sleeping. He looks like an angel. He is wearing a hospital gown and is connected to all different kinds of machines with weird sounds and numbers. It is scary. The beeping of the machines and the fluctuating numbers on the screens are overwhelming for Majesty.

Doctor Ogobuwu informs her he will discharge Arthur in a few days. He was placed on some medication, and they wish to see how he reacts to it so that they will keep him for observation.

The doctor exits the room and wishes them all the best.

She rushes over to her husband and kisses him on his forehead. She holds his hands and cries uncontrollably. Stephany walks over to her and touches his hands. She hugs her friend and provides her with the comfort she needs.

She is happy he pulled through but knows she has to ensure he maintains a healthy lifestyle going forward. This means a change of diet and slowing down on the business's day-to-day operations. She knows he will have to spend the night, so she makes herself comfortable on a futon, which the hospital staff has provided for her comfort.

She tells Stephany it is OK to leave and asks her to inform the others of the unfortunate ordeal. "They can come and visit him in the morning," she says as she prepares to get some rest. She thanks her for coming out and bids her farewell. Majesty calls the nanny, to find out how Demetre is doing as she had left him in tears.

The nanny answers the phone on the first ring. Majesty inquires about her son and is pleased to know that he is resting and calm. The house staff is concerned about their boss. She reassures them he is doing better and has just admitted been for observation. They end the call and say goodnight. Majesty stares at her husband and thanks God for answering her prayers.

She knows she has made a promise, but she has a few more things to take care of. Things she knows God won't be pleased about. After that, she is sure she will be ready.

CHAPTER 22

Discharged

Majesty is in deep slumber when a nurse walks in the room and startles her. "Good morning, Mrs. Bitting," she says in a pleasant voice. Majesty looks at the clock; it is 3 a.m. Her eyes are still a bit foggy, and she can feel how tired she is from not being well-rested.

"I will be taking Mr. Bitting's vitals. Don't mind me, you can go back to bed," says the nurse calmly as she walks over to his bed. Majesty is anxious to see how her husband is progressing, so she curiously watches as the nurse does her rounds. She carefully listens to his heart with her stethoscope and takes his blood pressure using a digital machine. She writes down all the numbers. She is a pleasant older lady. She asks Majesty if she needs anything and reassures her that her husband is doing fine.

Majesty asks, "How are his vitals?"

She replies, "His blood pressure and heart rate are a bit high, but that's normal because he just had surgery. He just needs to get some more rest." She removes the almost empty IV fluid bag and replaces it with a new one.

She says, "I will keep monitoring him to see how he is progressing." She pulls the machines out and closes the door behind her. Majesty walks over to her husband and kisses him on his forehead. She is happy he is improving but misses her husband's voice and touch. She needs him to wake up. She walks back to her futon, and not long after, she starts to doze off.

Approximately one hour into drifting off, she hears a groan. She thinks she is dreaming but realizes she isn't fully asleep. She jumps up and notices it is Arthur. He is waking up, seemingly in pain, but he is moving and groaning.

She rushes over to his bed in excitement. "Baby, baby." He slowly opens his eyes and gives her a faint smile; he also seems discombobulated. She holds onto his hand and says, "Baby?"

He answers, "Where am I? What happened?" She fights hard to hold back the tears, but she can't.

"Babe, you had a heart attack and are in the hospital."

He replies, "OK."

There is a red button above his bed marked "Ring for Assistance." She wants to get the nurse's attention, so she presses it.

One of the nurses rushes in. "Is everything all right?"

Majesty says, "Yes, nurse, my husband just woke up, and he is talking!" Majesty is now grinning from ear to ear as she proudly shares that her husband is now alert.

The nurse shares in her joy. "Wonderful news, Ms. Bitting. We will have the doctor in with him shortly."

"Baby, I am so scared," she says.

He says, "The last thing I remembered is playing with our son."

She responds, "Yes, and I heard you fall to the floor; I thought you were pranking and still playing with him, pretending you died, but then you weren't responding. And that's when we called 911."

Arthur opens his eyes and stares at his wife. He is surprised to hear all of this. He asks in disbelief, "A heart attack?"

Majesty nods in agreement. She continues, "You have a pacemaker installed. It increases your life expectancy, but you must change your lifestyle."

Mid-conversation, there is a knock on the door; it is the pleasant nurse who did his vitals earlier that morning.

"Good morning. How did you sleep, Mr. Bitting? How are you feeling?"

He replies, "A little too long is how I slept, nurse." They all chuckle. He continues, "I guess I am doing OK. My wife just told me I had a heart attack, and I am now wearing a pacemaker. I am used to wearing Versace, not a pacemaker, but it'll do." They laugh. Arthur is a charming and funny man. He finds the positive in everything, one of the many reasons Majesty loves him dearly.

The nurse confirms and says, "You're a lucky man. Yes, you had a heart attack." She checks his vitals again and tells him, "The doctor will see you later when he is doing his rounds." She asks if they need anything and tells them they can order from the cafeteria when the dietary aide visits with the menu.

Majesty starts to kiss and hug him again. She says, "Don't you ever scare me like that again."

He replies, "Tell that to my heart, baby. How is Demetre? I want to see him."

She calls Ms. B. and tells her to dress the baby and herself. She instructs her as to what to take from the house and to meet the driver in the garage.

The dietary aide enters the room with a menu board to take the breakfast orders. Shortly after, another nurse's assistant enters to assist Arthur to the bathroom to get him cleaned up for the day. After having breakfast and spending some alone time together, Demetre runs into the room. "Daddy!" Arthur is overjoyed to see his son.

Demetre tries to jump on Arthur, but Majesty cautions him, "Baby, Daddy isn't feeling too well, so we have to be gentle with him, OK?"

Demetre is disappointed but understands he must be gentle so Daddy can get better. While Demetre and his father enjoy some father-son bonding, Majesty goes to take a shower in Arthur's private bathroom. She requests fresh clothes from the nanny. In a few minutes, she emerges looking like a well-rested, clean wife. She hands her dirty items to the nanny. They say their goodbyes, and she leaves with their son.

Later that afternoon, Stephany, Alion, and Labron come to see their boss. They laugh, reminisce on the old days, joke, and play a few games. It is a good vibe. There is a knock on the door, and Doctor Ogobuwu appears. He is dressed in a green hat, scrubs, and blue disposable shoe coverings. His eyes have bags under them, and he looks like he is working the overnight shift.

He carefully discusses the progress with Arthur and Majesty. He tells them Arthur will be discharged today but should follow up with his primary care doctor. This is good news. Everyone is ecstatic. The husband, father, and boss will be home before sundown.

CHAPTER 23

Hair I Come!

Majesty has a few errands to run, including collecting her husband's medication at the pharmacy. While she waits, her eye is caught by a book, "Eating Healthy After a Heart Attack." This is perfect. She grabs the book and starts to browse through it quickly. She decides she will purchase it and give it to their chef as a guide on how to prepare Arthur's meals.

After buying the book, she jumps in her black Escalade and starts to read it:

- Eating healthily can help you recover and decrease the risk of further complications following a heart attack.
- A heart-healthy meal pattern focuses less on fatty food and more on vegetables, fruits, and whole grains.

She decides to go to the farmer's market to purchase ingredients for the meals she has in mind for Arthur. She is driving downtown when a white SUV, out of nowhere, swerves in front of her, cutting her off and almost causing her to hit a pole. She is livid. How dare this person? They don't even have the common decency to apologize. She speeds up to get close enough to the SUV and prepares to tell him a few colorful words. She notices the driver is busy on his phone arguing with someone and not paying any attention to the road. He could have killed her, or anyone else. Majesty needs to teach him a lesson. She follows behind him and is honking her horn.

He notices her in the rearview mirror, gives her the middle finger, and speeds away, unaware of who Comala Diana Facey Bitting is. As she approaches her destination, the sign "FARMER'S MARKET" is getting bigger and bigger. She drives into the parking lot, trying to secure a spot close enough to the entrance.

As she is about to park, she notices the same jerk that cut her off in the SUV is parked next to her. He exits the vehicle and disappears quickly into the crowd. She quickly parks and jumps out of her car, and heads to the vehicle. She is upset. First, he cut her off, then had the nerve to show her a middle finger. No, sir, not today! Majesty takes a brick used to secure a vendor's tarp safely and throws it through the passenger side window, causing the alarm to go off. It causes a big commotion, and people start to point in disgust and disagreement. She doesn't care.

She walks over to the vehicle and looks through the broken passenger window. She can see a wide range of bulk hair in the back of the car as if he sold or owned a salon. Majesty is a weave girl, and so she knows good hair when she sees it. There is human hair and wigs of all different types. She is excited but then quickly remembers she is mad! But now, she has gotten even. He got what he deserved.

She isn't going to let him ruin her day. She is on a mission to get healthy food for her husband.

She walks inside the busy farmer's market. The crowd of people talking sounds like a beehive. The vendors are advertising their produce, and music is playing at different stalls. The farmer's market has the freshest local produce, natural products, and uniquely handmade items. She picks berries, apples, oranges, carrots, potatoes, lettuce, tomatoes, etc. After shopping, Majesty is tired and ready to go home. She is heading back to the parking lot when she notices a crowd of people beside her truck and the SUV she damaged.

As she approaches her car, everyone is looking at her and pointing at her. *Snitches end up with stitches or in ditches*, she thinks to herself. But again, this is Majesty; she fears no one.

She quickly opens her trunk, places the items inside, and closes it. A lady points and shouts, "Sir that's the lady who threw the brick into your SUV."

The man turns around and walks up to Majesty and asks, "Did you fucking do this?"

"Yes, I fucking did. It should teach you a lesson not to road rage."

The man positions himself as if he is about to hit her. She quickly reaches for her gun in her pocketbook, points it at his head, and commands, "Take one more step, and I end your life right here, right now, in front of all these people."

The man freezes in his tracks and holds up his hand. Everyone runs into the market.

"Who do you think you are? You could have killed someone, and you have no remorse!" shouts Majesty.

The man quickly apologizes. He has no choice, with a gun pointed to his head. He says, "Ma'am, I am so sorry. I am in a rush. Please don't hurt me. I am going through a lot this morning." He continues, "I distribute hair for a living, and one of my containers is being held at the port, costing me a lot of money."

At this point, Majesty puts away her gun and is intrigued by his line of business.

He takes out a business card from his wallet and hands it to her.

She asks, "Are you talking unprocessed hair?"

He answers, "Yes, and I do wigs too. Have you ever heard about Remy hair, Brazilian hair, and Peruvian? A lot of famous people pay big bucks for them."

He walks over to his vehicle and tells her to follow him.

Majesty is so intrigued that she immediately calms down and is now investing in the wealth of knowledge the gentleman is sharing with her.

He reaches through the broken window, grabs one pack of the hair, and hands it to her. "Feel it. The quality is second to none." He says, "By the way, I am Steve."

She takes the weave from him and inspects it. Like her husband, Majesty is always thinking of ways to make extra money. "I am Majesty," she says, her eyes still fixated on the weave in her hand. In a very professional voice, she asks, "Let's say I am interested in retailing hair. What's the cost to get me a container of mixed unprocessed weave and wigs in every style and color? And what is the turnaround time?"

He says, "The hair is coming straight from the source, in India. On average, it takes two weeks once we order. The usual price is $50k, but for your trouble, I can source it for $40k. It is your job, however, to have it cleared once it enters the USA." He further says, "I have been in the game a long time. I can recommend a lot of clients to you. I have been in the business for years, and I still have trouble getting the container from the wharf. I am trying to get out of the business, if you're interested I will sell you my company and give you all my customer base."

She is very interested but needs to consult with her husband first. "Sounds good. I will speak with my husband and call you in the morning. We need to get the ball rolling ASAP." He takes her cell number. Majesty apologizes for throwing a brick in his car but warns him not to road rage anyone else. He, too, expresses his apologies. She smiles and nods; she jumps in her truck with the weave he gave her as a sample.

CHAPTER 24

Entrepreneurs

I t has now been a few days since Arthur has been home and getting well-needed rest. Majesty is excited to start his new diet journey. As she pulls into the driveway, the housekeeper greets and assists her in unloading the car. Majesty is more concerned with her recent encounter and cannot wait to tell her husband.

"Where is Mr. Bitting?" asks Majesty.

The housekeeper responds, "He is up and about and doing great. He is in the exercise room working out."

Majesty takes the medications out of the Escalade and goes to look for her husband.

He is busy running and sweating profusely on the treadmill in the home gym. He has his ear pods on and is in his zone.

She quickly leaves without him seeing her; she wants him to finish his exercise uninterrupted.

She goes upstairs to Demetre's bedroom. It is beautifully decorated and has blue walls with paintings of cars and farm animals. His name is written in red on the wall above his car bed. He has a play corner, and his toys are organized on the floor.

When he sees Majesty, he says, "Mommy, I wuv you."

She picks him up and kisses him. "I love you more, my baby."

She tells the nanny to take a break, and she will spend some time with her son. She puts his favorite movie on and cuddles with him until he falls asleep for his midday nap.

She sneaks out of his room as she doesn't want to wake him, and heads downstairs to see if her husband is done breaking a sweat.

Arthur greets her with a kiss and a hug. She playfully pushes him off and says, "Eeeewe baby, the shower is upstairs."

He continues to grab her and kisses her. She tries to dodge him but eventually concedes because she loves having her husband hold her, sweaty or not.

"How is your day going, my beautiful wife?" he asks.

She replies, "Babe, I almost shot a guy today."

Arthur laughs. "Baby, what do you mean shot a guy?"

She isn't laughing, "Babe, he almost ran me off the road, and when I blew my horn at him, do you believe he gave me the middle finger?"

Arthur keeps laughing. "He better be thankful you didn't shoot his middle finger off, or he would have to show someone his pinky next time."

They both laugh uncontrollably. Ms. B. is in earshot and chuckles a little.

Majesty recalls her encounter with Steve. "I went to the farmer's market, and guess who was there – the same culprit. His vehicle was parked next to mine, so I took the opportunity to bust the windows out of his car."

Arthur looks at her. "Woman, what am I going to do with you? What did I create?"

She continues, "When he came out, he was mad, and the snitches in the market kept pointing at me." She rolls her eyes. "So, he approached me and made a fist as if he wanted to hit me, so I had to defend myself. I pull out my pistol and say, 'Back the fuck up, or I will blow your head off.'"

Arthur is lost for words. She quickly dismisses that part of the conversation and says, "Anyways, turns out he ships hair from India, so now I want to do business with him."

Arthur cannot contain himself. "So babe, are you telling me this man almost ran you off the road, you broke his car window, you threatened him, and now he is your business partner? Comala Diana Facey Bitting, you are something else."

She laughs, "He is selling his business. He will give me all his customers and connections. Baby, I wear lots of weaves and wigs, which is not cheap. I know this will be very lucrative for us. We cannot go wrong in this venture. He will give me a good deal. His biggest problem is the wharf, getting his containers to clear."

"What do you think?"

He is a very supportive husband. "Just be careful, babe, but I support you if this is what you want."

She tells him she will take the $50,000 and have Stephany accompany her to meet with him as soon as possible to hear how much he is selling his company for and let him fill me in the details.

"I will inform our real estate lawyer about the new business plans." He says, "Baby, I don't want you to be driving with those duffle bags of money; it's too dangerous. Just write a check from the account, that's safer. Do what you need to do, but just be careful."

They both go to the kitchen and greet Chef Camfa. Majesty tells him about a new diet she wants for her husband.

Camfa replies, "I can put a vegetarian menu together for you, Mr. Bitting, and I will cook tofu in coconut milk with steamed vegetables for lunch." Majesty likes the sound of that.

They go upstairs for some private time. She whispers, "Baby, you scared me the other night. I thought I would have lost you. We must start doing things differently. I know you say we want to go international and start shipping heavier substances, but right now, you need to relax, heal, and let me take care of things." She continues, "The money from Romeo will be coming soon, as well as all the other products we sent out. The money generated from those transactions will keep us afloat for a while. "Club Vegas is doing great, not to mention the boutique," she says.

Arthur is very attentive when his wife speaks. He says, "You're right, baby."

She says, "All I need is for you to get well. I will take care of the operation of all the businesses from now on." She says, "I will give Labron, Alion, and Stephany an opportunity. I will give them enough money to start their own legitimate business. We will charge them just a small fee. We will get into hair distribution, distribute to stores all over, clean up the money, and just live as normal residents. I will have Stephany run the hair company."

He nods, agrees, and says, "Do what you think is best for the team, Comala. I trust you. I know they will be safe doing that!"

"Comala? You never called me that." She smiles at him. They both laugh.

"I can't wait to taste that tofu in coconut milk Camfa is making, and you need to take your medications," she demands.

"Baby, am I expected to take those pills for the rest of my life?" he asks.

She replies, "Yes, that's what the doctor says until your health drastically improves."

A delicious aroma is coming from the kitchen. They both get up and head in that direction.

They sit around the table, where Chef Camfa greets his bosses and places different delicacies on the table.

The fruits are fresh; the colors are bright and inviting. The meal is delicious.

After lunch, Arthur takes his medications and asks his wife to hire a personal trainer.

He knows he has to take care of himself and lets her take care of the business. He knows he needs to be healthy to be a good father to his son Demetre.

Later that evening, Labron, Alion, and Stephany call to check in on him.

Majesty invites the team over because she wants to tell them the new plan she has for the group.

When they arrive at the house, they all greet Arthur. They chat for a little and crack jokes, then they all gather around the dining table.

Majesty takes charge, and in a commanding voice, she says, "Well, everyone understands what is going on with our leader, and he needs to rest. We don't want him to be stressing and have another heart attack, so he has to take care of himself."

She goes on to say, "In the interest of everyone, and giving us all a break, we have decided that Labron and Alion both will get a head start to start their own business. Let us blend in with everyone and lie low for a while. We have enough money to stay off the grid." Turning her attention to Stephany, she says, "Stephany and I will get into the hair business. And distribute to local businesses."

Arthur chimes in, "Guys, I almost lost my life to a heart attack." He smiles and stares at everyone. "After all the stuff I do, a heart attack?" He laughs and shakes his head. They all laugh with him. He continues, "Majesty's plan sounds good. I think it's the best thing for us as a team right now."

Labron says, "That's not a bad idea. I know you're not well, Arthur, and you must take it easy from now on. Majesty is super smart and organized. We will be fine."

"Alion, what business will you go into?" Arthur asks.

He replies, "A used car dealership."

Arthur asks, "Labron, what kind of business?

Labron answers, "I can cook. A restaurant," shaking his head and smiling.

Stephany is happy. She loves working with her boss, Majesty. This is a great opportunity for her. They all eat dinner.

Arthur gives them his blessing and wishes them good luck.

CHAPTER 25
Boss Lady

ajesty is now in charge, and she has things to do. She promised to help everyone start their business, so she goes online looking for spots to open a new restaurant and a car dealership. She comes across a location for rent. She dials the phone number. The phone rings.

"Hello," an older man answers at the other end of the phone.

"Hello," she says. "I am interested in the location on South Sefie Street. I am planning to open a dealership. How much is it going for?"

The man answers, "I am Mr. Brown, and the asking price is eight thousand dollars per month. To move in, the requirements are first, last, and security deposit, a total of twenty-four thousand dollars."

He tells her a dealership was there before, and the location is already set up for such a business. He tells her she can view the property within an hour if she wants to. She quickly agrees.

She calls Alion and tells him to meet her at the address in an hour.

She tells Arthur what she is doing and her plans with Alion. She travels with $300,000 in a large bag. She knows her husband doesn't want her to be carrying that kind of money with her, but she locks it in the trunk of her truck. She separates the $24,000 in an envelope to pay for the spot if he likes it.

She arrives at the location and immediately notices it is in a great spot; it is busy. She arrives before Alion, and so she waits for him.

Majesty spots Alion's white BMW 5 series car in her rearview. She waits for him to pull up beside her.

They both exit their cars and greet each other.

Alion is five feet eleven inches tall and sports a bald head with a full beard. He is wearing full black and poised for business.

They are both scrutinizing the place as an older man exits the building. "Majesty?" Mr. Brown asks. Mr. Brown reaches out his hand as a gesture.

She nods and gives him a firm handshake.

"This is my brother Alion; he will be conducting business here."

The two gentlemen exchange handshakes.

She asks Alion, "Do you like this spot?"

Alion replies, "Yeah, location, location, location, it is ideal."

Mr. Brown says, "You're right. The location is great, plus we just renovated and did some painting. Come let me show you around."

Mr. Brown looks weary. He is obese and walks with a limp.

"I operated a car dealership here for twenty years," he says. "I'm getting old and was diagnosed with cancer last year. I must take it easy, so I am retiring and renting it. People still come here to buy cars as they don't know I am out of business, which would benefit you. I reassure you that this is a great spot."

He takes them indoors and shows them to the receptionist's desk. A closed-door private office space is at the back of the room. In that room, there is a big screen showcasing the cameras all over; they can see every angle inside and outside the building.

Alion gives Majesty his approval with a nod.

Majesty is ready to get down to business. She asks, "When can we set up shop?"

Mr. Brown replies, "If you make your payments today, you can start whenever you desire. I can give you an additional two months to set up and start operations officially."

Alion is intrigued. He asks, "Do you have connections at the auction for bringing in the vehicles?"

Mr. Brown replied, "Yes, my partner still runs the auction. He can supply you with what you need. I can make the connection for you. His name is Jake."

"Jake will get the specific vehicles you like, put them away, and send them here on a towaway dolly trailer. It can transport fifteen vehicles at a time. This is the easiest, quickest, most convenient way, not to mention affordability."

Majesty says, "OK, sounds good. Alion, do you want this location?"

"Yes, sis, I love it. Let's give it a go," he answers with excitement.

She smiles and asks Mr. Brown, "What if I want to purchase this property? How much are you willing to sell for?"

Mr. Brown raises his brows; he has a look of excitement on his face. He thinks to himself, *Did I just hit the jackpot?* He does not hesitate to quote them a price. He replies, "One-point two million."

In a very casual tone, Majesty says, "OK," she writes him a check for the amount and hands it to him.

Mr. Brown sits at the desk and examines the check. He is baffled at how easy it is for him to sell his shop at a cash price. They exchange their lawyers' information to make the transfer of title.

He takes a paper from the pouch he is carrying, writes her a receipt, and hands it to her.

He makes a call to his lawyer. Shortly after he hangs up, he tells her he can have the document sent by email for her and her lawyer to review and sign. He tells them a little history about the location.

Mr. Brown then picks up his phone and dials Jake.

"Hello, hey, my brother," says Mr. Brown in a happy voice after Jake answers.

Mr. Brown listens to his reply.

"Hey family," Mr. Brown says, "I got Mr. Alion and Ms. Majesty here. They just bought my location. They need some help getting vehicles in from the auction. Can you hold on? I will let you speak to him."

He hands the phone to Alion.

"Hello, boss man," says Alion to the man on the other end of the phone.

Majesty interrupts. "Choose the vehicles you want so he can deliver them here. The sooner, the better."

Alion pushes the speaker button so everyone in the room can hear the conversation with Jake.

An older gentleman's voice says, "Let me get a pen to take down the order. Go ahead now."

Alion says, "I need the 2022 years. Five Corollas, five Camrys, five Hondas, six Mercedes-Benz trucks, six Mercedes-Benz cars, five Lexus trucks, four Lexus cars."

The man on the phone replies, "Four hundred thousand dollars."

Alion looks to Majesty for approval.

Majesty says, "I only have three hundred thousand dollars in my car right now. I will have the balance delivered in the morning if that is OK with you."

Jake says, "You can leave the money with Mr. Brown. I will get it from him. I can have the vehicles delivered to you there. I need three to four weeks to complete the order for you."

Alion is so excited he hugs and thanks Majesty for giving him this great opportunity.

He walks with her to her truck.

She asks, "Alion, are you sure this is something you can manage? You will need to hire some sales associates, a receptionist, and a finance manager to approve the customers' loans. You need to get on top of advertisements, flyers, and business cards to start up the business and do some marketing."

He replies, "I will make you proud, Majesty."

Majesty reaches into the passenger side of the vehicle and grabs the bag of money. They both walk back inside.

Alion hands the large bag of money to Mr. Brown.

Mr. Brown counts the money, and when he is finished, he places the money back into the bag. He holds on to the bag, walks them to the back of the building, and shows them around.

He tells Majesty he will call her when the check is clear. She interrupts him. "I can give you the additional hundred thousand dollars in a check for Jake."

He says, "OK, that can work."

She reaches into her pocketbook, writes the check for the $100,000 balance for Jake, and hands it to him.

Mr. Brown stares at the check and, places it in his wallet, and writes Majesty a receipt.

He tells them to call him if they need anything. He walks outside with the huge bag and leaves the location.

When Mr. Brown drives off, Majesty says to Alion, "You will pay me four thousand dollars monthly for rent."

Alion is happy with the idea. He says, "Are you sure? Majesty, remember one of the vehicles is over thirty thousand dollars."

She replies, "You got this. I just want to see you succeed." Majesty handed him the $25,000. To start getting his paperwork together. She is so happy to see him so happy.

CHAPTER 26
Food Is Life

Majesty is on a great path to ensuring everyone is settled and making their own money. She has to now focus on getting Labron into the restaurant business. She starts her morning by caring for Arthur, ensuring he takes his medication and has his breakfast after he goes swimming with his trainer. Checking on Demetre and loving up on him before she goes back to handling her business. Back to the drawing board, she goes into the office and searches for locations appropriate for housing a restaurant. She comes across a location in Portland West, downtown LA. She dials the number in the listing.

As the phone rings, a man answers the other end of the phone. "Hello," says Majesty, "I am interested in the restaurant spot you have for rent in Portland West."

The man replies, "Sure! It is still available."

She asks, "How much are you renting this spot for?"

He replies, "Seventy-five hundred dollars per month, and I want first, last, and security to move in and one-hundred-fifty for a background check." They have a brief conversation, trying to arrange a convenient time for viewing. They both agree on the time and end the call. She immediately calls Labron and asks him to meet at the location in an hour. She gives him the address.

In a matter of forty-five minutes, she arrives at the location. When she arrives, Labron is parked and waiting for her. He is serious about business. They both emerge from their vehicles and greet each other. They look around, but the man she spoke to on the phone is nowhere to be found. The place seems to have been closed for a while, but it is a prime location. She redials his phone. He answers on the first ring.

He answers, "Hello?"

"Hi, this is the lady you spoke to about the restaurant. I am at your location."

He replies, "I am on my way. The traffic is very awful coming over. I am fifteen minutes away, my deepest apologies."

She replies, "OK, see you soon."

They use the opportunity to start viewing the building and its environs. They are amazed at how busy the highway is. It is just at one of the exits. "The location is perfect," says Labron.

Majesty agrees with a nod and grin, and they bump fists.

A silver pickup enters the parking lot and parks beside them. A man and woman exit the truck; they are an older couple. The lady is beautiful, with grey strands in her head full of hair. The couple approaches them and extend handshakes.

"Hello, I am Majesty, and this is my brother Labron." The old man and his wife shake hands with them.

"We're the Johnsons," says the woman.

She leads them to the door, and they enter the building.

Mrs. Johnson says, "This is three thousand square feet." She points. "This is the hostess area, seating area, and then we have a swinging door that leads to the kitchen." There is a huge metal table in the center of the kitchen. It also has a commercial fridge, double sinks, an industrial stove, and a microwave. Pots and pans are neatly placed in order.

She directs them to the lavatories for staff and guests. There is also a manager's office. "This is a large space. I love it," says Majesty. In a confident voice, she asks, "Are you selling this spot?"

Mr. Johnson says, "Yes, we are selling everything here for one million."

He looks at his wife for her approval. She nods and agrees with her husband.

Majesty says, "I will buy the building."

She writes them a check for the total amount and tells them her attorney will contact them regarding the transference of the title and deed.

Mrs. Johnson writes them the receipt and hands them the keys for the property. She gives them a few ideas on how to decorate the dining area and bar. After completing the transaction, they exit the building.

After they leave, Majesty tells Labron he will take control of the restaurant and pay her a monthly rent of $500 starting in seven months.

He is so surprised. "Majesty, five hundred dollars, are you sure? That's nothing. I can more than pay that."

He is so excited for the opportunity.

Majesty gives him a few ideas herself, and she hands him $50,000 to start the business.

She asks him, "What kind of restaurant will you open?"

He replies, "High end. I want to create a classy and sophisticated ambiance."

She agrees. "You can do music and live bands. This will be the new spot on a Saturday night in LA," exclaims Majesty. Labron is so excited to start this new venture.

He tells her he likes the name "La Morchette Bistro."

She replies, "That's a sexy name. Make it into a fancy, lavish, and romantic spot, fresh flowers daily, tasteful artwork, classical music, satin tablecloths, napkins, and valet parking."

They both smile as they envision the setting.

He agrees with her on the idea of the restaurant and tells her he will register the name and start planning for the grand opening.

She offers, "Contact Sam, who manages Club Vegas nightclub, and get his advice with the operation because that's his field of expertise."

He agrees.

She makes the necessary arrangements and sets up a meeting with both parties.

Labron values Majesty's opinion, and he needs her input. He wants her advice on the color scheme to use. She allows him to make all the decisions.

"Make your budget and let me know so I can run it by Arthur. I know you will need silverware, plates, wine glasses, menus, and promotional materials." She continues, "For the liquor, I already have the connection from Club Vegas Night, so just put it all together, and I will go over it with Arthur."

He hugs her and thanks her for the opportunity.

He walks her to her car. Before she drives off, she says confidently, "Labron, you got this," and smiles.

CHAPTER 27

New New

Alion's pre-owned car dealership is coming together. He decides to register his business under the name "Blaze Pre-owned Cars." He gets the required business licenses and permits and ensures he is operating within the law of the state.

All the vehicles he ordered are steadily arriving. In no time, the lot is looking great, and he is ready to open his doors. Back in the day, when he lived in Florida, Alion worked as a sales associate. Craig, his old boss, made an impact on him, motivating and educating him on how to market and sell cars. He reaches out to Craig and asks him to move to California. He will provide a company car and a huge bonus. Craig gladly accepts.

When Craig arrives, he is impressed by how the dealership is set up. The vehicles are neatly parked in order, model by model. The lobby is neatly decorated and very comfortable for customers.

Alion is very proud of himself and this new venture of his own. Having his old boss, whom he admires, means a lot to him. He leads him to his office; he likes the setting as it reminds him of how his office is set up in Florida.

He sits at his desk for the first time, and they start to talk about the core of how to make Blaze Pre-owned Cars become the best in town,

Craig asks, "What's the budget for marketing and advertising?"

Alion replies, "A hundred thousand."

Due to his experience in the field, Alion is confident in his ability to lead and manage the day-to-day operations of the establishment. "I will pay you a weekly salary of two thousand dollars and a percentage from every car that is sold, full insurance and pension benefits," he says. Craig is super excited and is ready to embark on the new adventure and build Blaze Pre-owned.

"OK, let's get the ball rolling, Craig. I have faith in you and what you can do with this place. We will start fresh in the morning."

The following morning, Craig arrives early and is ready to work. Alion arrives one hour later. Alion invests a lot in marketing. At this point, commercials on the radio and television can be heard repeatedly. The phone lines are going off the hook, with people requesting job interviews.

Craig oversees the operations. He quickly gets to work and starts setting appointments for interviews. They need a fully competent staff to serve the customers efficiently. After several days of interviews and shortlisting candidates, they hire two bilingual receptionists, three finance managers, and seven sales associates. Blaze Pre-owned Cars is ready for business.

CHAPTER 28
Coming Together!

A lion owns the Blaze Pre-owned Cars dealership. Labron owns La Morchette Bistro restaurant. Majesty is happy the team is all settling into their new lives and never has to kill or hide from the police anymore. She still needs to get the hair business going. She will give Stephany the same opportunity she gave Alion and Labron. She dials Steve's number.

She needs to find out how much he is selling the weave business for.

"Hello, my friend Steve, this is Majesty. How are you?"

She listens to his reply.

"Great, I want to know how much you are selling your business for?"

He replies, "Seven hundred thousand dollars. I will give you all my weave, hair products, and connections."

She replies, "OK, when can I see you?"

He replies, "I will be at my establishment in two hours."

She says, "OK, I will see you."

Majesty calls her bank, informing them that some big transfers will be coming out of her account. She gives the customer care rep the amounts, and then she hangs up. She dials Stephany's number and tells her to get dressed; she will be picking her up. She recalls how she met

Steve, and she informs her of the planned meeting with him in LA in the afternoon.

After she hangs up the phone, she researches his company listed on the business card. She likes the reviews he is getting on his website. She feels hopeful.

She gets dressed, kisses her husband, and jumps in her truck. She goes to Stephany's apartment to pick her up. They both look and smell amazing.

When she gets in the vehicle, she turns on the music, and they jam to the song on the radio.

She goes to the address on the business card. When they arrive, they go to the front desk, and a lady leads them to Steve's office.

She says, "Hi Steve, how are you? This is my cousin Stephany."

He replies, "Hey, Majesty, hi, Stephany." He takes them to a room and shows them the various styles, colors, wigs, and hair products. He says, "Let me give you a little history on weave.

"Human weave is a natural hair extension that is attached to human hair by sewing, gluing, or clipping. These weaves will last weeks at a time, so my customers keep returning for the quality." He gives them extensive details.

"Extensions are what we offer to add volume and length to a person's real hair. Weave is a different type of extension that creates a thicker, longer, more glamorous look. Weft is a bundle of extensions in which women sew tracks to reinforce the stitches.

"The hairstyles we provide are raw Indian Remy, deep wave, straight, closure, bulk hair, lace front wigs. Every color, you name it, and wigs."

Stephany asks, "This hair is unprocessed raw virgin hair?"

He replies, "Absolutely, one hundred percent great quality."

Majesty is impressed.

He gives them a tour, shows them how the business operates, and gives them a list of client information. He shows them the annual gross profit, and it is great.

Majesty asks, "With seven hundred thousand dollars, I am getting this storefront and all the weaves, wigs, and hair products down to the chairs, table, computers, and papers." They all laugh.

Steve answers, "Yes," and nods his head.

Majesty writes him a check for the business and tells him her lawyer will be contacting his lawyer for the transfer of title.

He writes her a receipt, and they shake hands.

She asks him to show her how to make the order for the container of weave and wigs.

She takes out her credit card, and he shows them how to place the order.

He tells them, "In two to four weeks, you can go to Customs and collect your shipment. Majesty," he reiterates, Customs will be your biggest challenge."

As promised, he gives her a list of clients who love the products he offers.

Weeks after the shipment arrives, her phone rings.

She answers, "Hello?"

"Hello." A male voice is on the other end of the phone.

"Hello, is this Comala Bitting?"

She pauses for a minute. Who knew her legal name?

"Yes, this is she."

"This is Customs and Border Patrol. My name is Mr. Mark Williamson. Your container was just unloaded off the cargo. You need to come to the wharf as soon as possible."

She says, "OK, I am on my way. Is everything OK?"

The rough-voiced man replies, "When you get here, I will explain."

"Stephany, we must go to the port. Customs held on to the shipment," she says. "Steve told me this is the biggest problem we will have. I must find a way to fix it."

They rush to the truck and speed off. They are greeted at the office door by an older, well-polished lady, who leads them to Mr. Williamson. "Right this way, he is expecting you," she says in a high-pitched tone.

When they arrive at his office, they see his name on his door, Manager Mr. Williamson. They walk into his office; he has a desk with tons of scattered papers. He seems like a very disorganized manager. He tells them to have a seat.

He asks, "Which one of you is Comala?"

Majesty responds, "I am, but please call me Majesty."

He says, "Thanks for coming after such short notice.

"We found some illegal narcotics in your container. We have no choice but to seize it until we complete an investigation."

Majesty is shocked. She knows she had put a pause on drug shipping, so how is this possible?

She asks, "What?"

By the time she is ready to ask another question, his cellphone rings. He looks at his phone and takes a deep breath. He says, "Ladies, this is an important call that I must take. Please excuse me." He gets up from his desk, goes into the next room, and says, "Hello."

He doesn't know his phone is so loud they can hear the person on the other end. The lady on the phone says, "Mr. Williamson, your daughter is unable to finish this semester. We cannot accept any more excuses from you. Her fees are well overdue."

"Mrs. Michelle Dennis, please, I will get it to you.'"

She cuts him off abruptly. "The tuition must be paid immediately. Nichola cannot return to school to finish her doctorate at this time. She cannot return to campus until the sixty-five thousand dollars is paid in full."

The call ends, and he returns to his desk looking disappointed and dejected.

He takes a seat and continues in a soft voice, "Where were we, ladies? Can I get the receipt for your container order and your ID?"

Majesty reaches into her purse, hands him $70,000 in an envelope, and says, "I wish Dr. Nichola Williamson all the best in her endeavors. Take care of your daughter, Mr. Williamson. Call me when you conclude the investigation for my shipment."

Majesty is smart. She is caring, too, but she knows exactly what she is doing.

Tears roll down his cheeks. He jumps from his chair and hugs her. He says, "I have been working at this place for 15 years, and I can hardly cover my bills. My daughter has two more years to finish up her studies. This money will help me out a great deal."

He calls the college, and they put him through to the bursar's office.

He says, "Mrs. Michelle Dennis, I will have the money no later than today. I am going to make payment in full."

He hangs up the phone and turns his attention to Majesty. "Ms. Bitting, you will never have a problem with your shipment ever again." He writes his cell number down on a white piece of paper and tells her, "If you need anything don't hesitate to call me. Give me until tomorrow. I will fix the error in the computer. You can pick up your container any time after 2 p.m. tomorrow."

Majesty and Stephany know they have created a solid link. Everyone leaves the meeting happy.

CHAPTER 29
Goodbyes

Adisha reminisces about his friend, Badaz. He lies on his back on a high-quality, well-constructed mattress that provides him with the best sleep surface to meet his physical needs.

He stares at the ceiling of his master bedroom, reminiscing on the fun times he had with his best friend, who was his only family. All the dangerous experiences they had killing, partying, traveling, etc. They almost lost their lives many times, and he would do it all over again.

Badaz's death plagues his mind. "What these people did to my best friend is unforgivable. The way they beheaded him, packaged his head, and sent it to the Asylum Night Club was sick."

What a shame the police found his body six miles away from the club, buried in a shallow grave. The funeral home had their work cut out for them. They had to sew his head back on his body for a proper open-casket funeral. To the Faceoff Crew, it was the biggest disrespect anyone could ever imagine.

If Badaz was alive and it was the other way around, he would make sure those motherfuckers paid for my murder, he thinks to himself.

He blames himself for his best friend's murder and feels he should have been there to help him. How could he even allow him to be alone?

"I must make these people pay for his murder. He took care of me while I was incarcerated and cared for my father. I must kill someone in honor of him." He is now the new boss of Asylum Night Club. He has a team to lead and a reprisal to conduct. There is a lot of pressure on him to make abrupt decisions. He now runs the operation of Badaz's businesses and must ensure he stays on top of everything.

Badaz's body is still in the morgue. The forensic pathologist is waiting for the police to give the green light to finish their investigation.

Adisha thinks to himself, *I won't say anything to the cops because I know who did this, and I don't want them going to jail. I want them dead.*

He takes his cellphone off the bedside table and dials the funeral home's phone number.

"Hello, this is LAD Funeral Homes. How may I help you?" a very pleasant female answers.

"Hi, this is Adisha, calling again about Badaz Brooks, who was murdered. He was decapitated. Please tell me I can give him an open-casket funeral service," he wails.

"Yes, we placed his head back on his body. You can have the service the way you and your family desire. The police gave us the green light to release his body, now that the autopsy is complete. You can now start preparing to bury him."

Adisha is relieved. It is a long time coming. "What is the cost of the package?" he asks.

"The payment of twenty thousand dollars will be due as soon as possible. For that package, we will give him a funeral plot. We will also need a tuxedo, a pair of shoes, and some socks for him. Do you have a minister to commit the body that will lay to rest at our cemetery?"

He interrupts her. "I don't have a minister. Is that something you offer? We would love to get this handled by Saturday at the latest."

She answers, "The package I am offering you covers everything. The wake will be here on Friday from 5 p.m. to 9 p.m., and the burial will be the following day. On the day of the funeral, we will provide one hundred programs. If possible, we need some pictures of the deceased and information about him for his obituary.

"After the funeral, you will receive his death certificate. The body will be at the church, and the minister will also accompany the procession to the cemetery on Thirty-fourth Street."

"That sounds perfect. I will drop off his tux, the funds, and some pictures for you."

He thanks her and goes into planning mode. He heads to the Asylum Night Club location. When he arrives, he instructs the guard to tell everyone he needs a meeting with them in his office. When he gets to Badaz's office, now his, he sits down, grabs a notepad, and begins to scribble details about his funeral date and cost.

A few moments later, there's a knock at the door, and he invites the people to come in. All twenty men in the crew walk in, one at a time, and find a space to stand.

Adisha addresses them. "OK, I know you all are sad that Badaz is dead, and his remains are still at the morgue after so long. I can assure you all it's because there's been an ongoing investigation. They just found his body and gave the funeral home the green light to conduct the funeral service." Adisha reassures the group, "I know this is hard for all of you. Our boss, Badaz, is not here with us anymore." He wipes the tears from his eyes. He continues, "We will get revenge. Until then, let us pay our final respects to the boss man and give him the sendoff he deserves. Once we have that taken care of, then we take care of the other business."

He starts to delegate and give each person responsibilities; some are in charge of the tuxedo, others are in charge of transportation, etc. He confirms the date and time with each member and ensures everything is under control for the weekend.

Binns is more interested in revenge. He asks, "Do you know who did it?"

"Yes, he had a meeting with the Bittings a few weeks before he was murdered, the couple who owns Club Vegas. I am pretty sure they have everything to do with his death."

He replies, "What about Top Dog Crew, Bellevue Crew, and the Choppa Crew? He had beefs with everyone, anyone could have murdered him."

"That's true, but the Bittings disrespected him, and even if it's not them, they deserve to be shaken up, to teach them who the real gangsters are."

The wake and funeral are fast approaching. The wake is a short and intimate event. The turnout is great.

The following morning is the funeral. Badaz lies peacefully in a white casket for the mourners to pay their last respects. A large bouquet of flowers is on the casket, and about one dozen are on the podium. It is beautifully decorated. A large photo of him is on an easel on the podium. He is wearing a white suit and sunglasses. He has swag even in death. He looks as if he is sleeping.

Most people are wearing black, and the atmosphere is somber. Adisha has sunglasses on as well, trying to hide his tears. He is so sad and angry to see Badaz's lifeless body.

The pastor enters the room, and everyone is quiet. You can hear a few sobs here and there. The funeral is mournful, and his friends and family bask in the memories of the good times they had. After the ceremony, the pallbearers make their way to the casket and carry out their duty with grace and honor. The procession involves a motorcade to his final resting place.

After the ceremony, the repast is held at the club. Once that is over, Adisha calls a meeting to discuss the plans to find his killers and avenge him.

Before the men enter the office, Adisha places three duffle bags of money, cocaine, and jewelry in the closet in the office for safekeeping.

"I need one of you to get me these fuckers, and if we can't get them directly, we must start attacking their team members, one by one!" he shouts in rage. "By the way, how did Badaz even end up in a car with them? He didn't drive his car; it is still parked in the VIP area. If he didn't trust them, he would not go with them, nor would he go by himself if he wasn't sure." He walks around, pacing back and forth, waiting for answers.

Kirk feels so guilty he can't make eye contact with anyone in the room; nor can he say anything. He must maintain his composure and pretend he is concerned and upset. Occasionally he chimes in, "Those motherfuckers must die!" He feels guilty because he is the one who helped Stephany by letting her know when he was at the club and how to get close to him. It was perfectly orchestrated. *This is a dangerous game. I must stay away from her. These people will kill me and her if they find out I had anything to do with his death,* Kirk thinks to himself.

It is getting serious; the funeral is over, and now the Bittings are the target.

CHAPTER 30
Long Run, Short Catch

I t's the grand opening, finally, and Arthur and Majesty want to be the first customers. They are looking at a Benz Jeep as they want to support Blaze Pre-owned cars.

"How much is this Benz truck?" asks Arthur.

A sales associate replies, "Seventy-five thousand dollars." He attends to them and talks them through the process. They go for a test drive and decide to buy the truck in cash to support him.

Alion is so excited to see his vision coming to fruition.

More customers are coming to see the vehicles that they have to offer. The place is so busy with customers driving in and out excited to see the grand opening of Blaze.

Alion is on top of his game. After the Bittings complete their transaction, he asks, as a boss, "How is the service?"

Arthur replies, "It is an easy process, and that sales associate has a lot of experience in sales. He is very good and very professional."

Majesty adds, "The process is quick, and the finance manager is very professional and worked very fast." Alion feels proud to hear that everything went smoothly.

* * *

Adisha and Binns drive into the car park. They hear the commercial playing on the radio all day and decide to check out this new spot. Adisha needs a second truck, and the commercial for Blazing Pre-owned sounds so inviting and has amazing deals. Little do they know, this place is connected to the people who were responsible for the death of his best friend.

Adisha recognizes Majesty and Arthur from a distance. Not far from them, he spots Stephany, who was at the club the night of Badaz', disappearance, talking to him. Then he spots Alion and Labron.

"This is perfect," he says to himself. "It must be a sign to have them all in one place. It is the perfect place to execute his plan." But he thinks, *I can't do this now. We have to plan and regroup and then attack.* He sits in his vehicle and observes each one of them.

He says, "Binns, it looks like these fools own this spot. They are taking over everything."

At this point, Adisha is not even thinking about who is responsible for his best friend's death. He wants everyone dead.

He says, "We will follow one of them tonight and torture that bitch. I will get to the bottom of this, and he must give us the information we need." He says in an angry tone, "Badaz is dead. I can't wait to get my hands on one of these pussy ass niggas. By the way, the one dressed in the suit looks like he owns this place. We will get him later. He will tell us everything we need to know if they had anything to do with Badaz's murder."

Binns replies, "Boss, those motherfuckers murdered our boss, they had every reason to do it. He called them in a meeting to share their profits, and they declined the boss' offer, and you know Badaz wasn't happy about that."

Adisha and Binns wait in the car, watching every move Arthur, Majesty, Stephany, Alion, and Labron make.

Adisha makes a few phone calls to set up the plan for that evening. They post up in the parking lot before everyone leaves. They blend in with the other customers and drive outside, waiting patiently for their victims to leave. Adisha has a plan, and the group is ready to execute it.

CHAPTER 31
Reprisal

Alion is elated. He is proud of himself. He goes to his office and reminisces on how he was so poor as a kid and now he owns this dealership. His mind quickly runs to Roxanne, to their last conversation; she told him she had missed her period. He says to himself, "I was so busy getting the dealership ready for opening, I didn't even call my boo, Roxanne. I will give her a call later tonight when I get home."

All the sales associates and finance managers are busy closing all the deals for the day and preparing to leave.

At the end of the work shift, the store has sold fifteen vehicles. That is a record deal, one they must top the next day. It is 10 p.m., and Craig and Alion sit down to review the day's sales and prepare the list of vehicles they need to order based on the current inventory. Everyone has left except the security and the two gentlemen. After concluding the day's sales and placing the order, they begin to make their way to the exit.

Both men walk out and close the doors behind them. They say their goodbyes and go in different directions. Alion is blasting the music in his pickup truck. He is over the moon, dancing and singing, celebrating his accomplishments. He is so distracted with the thoughts of today's sale that he doesn't notice the vehicle trailing him.

Suddenly, he remembers that he is out of a few things at home, so he pulls off to the corner store to grab a few things. He has been so busy lately with the dealership he forgot to take care of things at home. He parks and walks into the corner store. Alion grabs a cart and walks in the aisles to get the items he needs. He picks up bread, milk, juices, water, and eggs, and heads to the cashier. The store clerk rings up his items and gives him the total. He pays with his credit card, and she hands him his bags and receipt.

When he returns to his vehicle with the grocery bags, Binns, dressed in full black and a ski mask, walks up behind him, points a gun to his head, and orders him to get in the truck parked alongside his vehicle.

He is so frightened he has no choice but to get in the truck with the man. He has been in these situations before, but he would be the one making the order. He fears for his life, so he complies.

"Who the fuck are you, and what do you want?" Alion shouts. He drops the bags.

"Shut the fuck up," Binns replies. He picks up the grocery bags and puts them in the truck.

"Give me your keys, asshole," Binns says. Alion hands him the truck keys.

"Yow, if you want money, I can get you money. Let me go," replies Alion.

Binns commands, "Get in." The door slides open. Kirk is waiting inside. As he gets in, they use a black cloth to cover his face. The cloth has a weird odor, and Alion passes out.

Binns jumps in Alion's vehicle and follows behind Adisha as he drives down a dirt path to an abandoned house. The house is empty, with board floors and cracked windows.

Kirk and Binns take unconscious Alion out of the truck and tie him up on a metal chair in the middle of the room. They bind his hands and feet and uncover his eyes.

Adisha is angry. In a very commanding tone, he says, "Torture him until he tells us everything because we will do the same thing to him what they did to Badaz. We will send his head to his dealership."

"Wake up," says Adisha, while he slaps Alion with a gun. Binns gives

Alion a hard punch in his face. Alion wakes up with a fright. He goes in and out of consciousness.

Binns strikes him another blow; this one wakes him up.

He is discombobulated. He looks around and sees four men standing around him and a bright light in his eyes.

Bewildered and obviously in pain, he tries to move; in that moment, he realizes he is restrained. Binns gives him another blow; at this point, he can taste blood. "You and your friends killed my boss and had the audacity to send his head to us!"

Alion suddenly knows who these people are and knows this isn't good.

He says to himself, *Fuck, I am dead. I refuse to be a snitch. I will take one for the team if I must.* He coughs and replies in a weak tone, "I don't know what you're talking about. Who the fuck is your boss?"

"Oh, so now you want to play dumb?" Adisha says to Kirk, "Tase his ass."

He shoves the taser onto Alion's neck and asks, "Who killed my boss?"

Alion lies, "I don't know what you are talking about."

They continue to use the taser, and with each shock Alion shrieks in pain. Every question they ask, he denies having any knowledge.

Adisha is getting impatient and needs answers. He punches him and breaks his nose. At this point, Alion is about to lose consciousness; the excruciating pain is getting to him, but he refuses to talk.

Alion asks, "OK, you are not talking?" He instructs one of the men to cut off his fingers until he decides to talk, and so they do. For each finger he loses, he cries in agony but remains loyal. Alion swallows and takes a deep breath. Blood gushes as his pinky falls off.

"Fuck you, I don't know what you are talking about," he lies again. Alion is sweating profusely. Binns cuts another finger off, and he screams.

Kirk asks, "Adisha, are you sure this man and his friends killed Badaz? He lost two fingers, he has a broken nose, a busted face, and he is not talking."

CHAPTER 32

Horrors

Majesty jumps from her sleep, panicking. She has chills and can feel a sharp pain in her head from the sudden jerk. Her hands are shaking, and her heart is pounding; she hears her own heartbeat. She is looking around the room, feeling paranoid and afraid. She rubs her eyes, trying to make sense of her surroundings. She has the same nightmare again; this is the third night in a row. She quickly remembers when Bob and his friend murdered her parents. She whispers, "Mommy and Daddy, I miss you."

Arthur is sound asleep beside her. She looks at the clock; it is 3:39 a.m. She jumps out of bed, grabs her robe, and then goes to the kitchen for water. She can't understand why she is having this nightmare repeatedly. Why is this monster trying to kill her?

"This is so weird," she thinks to herself. She walks back to her bedroom, jumps back into bed, and cuddles up with her husband, still thinking about the dream until she goes back to sleep.

At 7 a.m., she finally wakes up. Arthur is already up with his trainer; she goes to the bathroom to get her day started. She can't shake the feeling from her dream last night but can't let it affect her daily routine.

She gets dressed and then checks on her son and ensures he is getting ready for school. When he sees her, he runs to her and hugs his mom. She plays with him for a little before heading to the breakfast table.

Arthur is already at the dining table. He kisses Demetre and joins them for breakfast. "Hey, son, how is school going?" asks Arthur.

Demetre replies, "Good, Daddy, I can say my ABCs now."

Arthur replies, "Oh! Can you? Let me hear you sing it," with a proud smile on his face.

Demetre sings, "A-B-C-D-E-F-G-H-I-J-K-Elemeno-Peeeee-Q-R-S-T-U-V-W-X-Y and ZZZZZZZ."

They clap for him at the table. Ms. B. hands Majesty his lunchbox, and they leave for the day.

She thinks, *Alion's dealership is open, Stephany is doing an amazing job with her weave business, and Labron's grand opening is this Friday. I am so proud of the team. They are going to do great.*

She is impressed with the vehicle her husband bought from Alion's dealership; it cost $75,000. It is everything the sales associate said and then some. She takes up her phone to call Alion to brag about her new truck.

His phone rings, but he doesn't pick up on the first ring. That is unlike him, but she thinks to herself, *He might be busy with the dealership. He will call me back in a few.*

She drops Demetre off at school and heads for the boutique. The store clerk greets her. "Hi, Ms. Bitting, how are you today?"

She answers, "I am doing OK, let me see the packages that you received yesterday,"

She leads her to the storeroom, points, and shows her the large boxes she received.

She opens one of the boxes and looks at the style to make sure it's the right color and size.

Customers are in the store looking at all the beautiful outfits they have to offer.

She goes into her office and is trying to balance the books when she hears her cellphone ringing. She says to herself, "That must be Alion returning my call."

When she looks at the phone, she sees it is Stephany.

She answers, "Hey, Stephany." Paying attention to what Stephany is saying over the phone, she pauses from her paperwork. "What?" Majesty asks in a frightened tone. "I tried to call him too, and he didn't pick up. Are you sure he didn't show up? How long have you been trying to call him?" Worried, she says, "I will meet you at his dealership."

She grabs the money in the safe and tells her workers she has an emergency and has to leave.

She hops in her truck and makes her way toward the dealership. She tries calling his cellphone again; no answer.

She thinks, *That is unusual. Alion just opened his business, and he is not answering his phone. Maybe he is at his house, but Stephany says she went there, and he is not there, and his vehicle is not in his parking space.*

She knows that crew members are always a target with the line of work they do to get all the money they have. It's not easy in this business; sometimes, they do things that are not right, so if something is out of the ordinary, it will raise a red flag.

She dials Arthur's phone number.

He answers, "Hello wife, how is your day going?"

She answers, "Baby, they say Alion didn't show up for work, and I tried calling him. Did you hear from him?"

He replies, "No, maybe he is out. Give it a few." He tries to reassure her that everything is OK.

She says, "OK, maybe you're right. I am meeting Labron and Stephany at his dealership. I will let you know once we get a hold of him, OK? He needs to know that now he is a business owner, he must show up at his place of business on time."

When she arrives at the dealership, Labron and Stephany are already there talking to Craig. She parks and heads in their direction.

"Did anyone get a hold of him? He is always on point; he always answers his cellphone; this is so out of his character." Majesty is obviously overly concerned.

Craig says, "We left here last night at around 10 p.m. together, and he told me that he may stop at the corner store for a few things. That is the last I heard from him."

Stephany says, "I am going back to his house and see if I missed anything when I was there. Labron, come with me."

They both hop in Stephany's truck and speed off to find Alion.

Craig and Majesty go inside his office to check the camera to see if there are any suspicious activities. They watch the footage a few times, and they notice when Craig and Labron drive off, but nothing strange meets their eyes.

Craig says, "I think we should call the police; I have a very bad feeling about this."

Majesty replies, "The police won't do anything. It has not even been 24 hours yet. Just give it a few more hours and see if he shows up."

Majesty's cellphone rings. It is Author.

She answers, "Hello, babe." She pauses and says, "No, this is weird, babe. You know he would never stay so long and not return any of our calls. He didn't show up to work. We know Alion. Stephany and Labron went back to his house. They will use the spare key and see if he got home last night. He is probably drunk, celebrating the opening of his dealership. I will let you know of any new developments."

I know all the enemies we have. When something is off, like not answering your phones and not showing up, it means something is wrong, she thinks to herself.

Arthur asks, "Where is his vehicle?"

She replies, "It's missing."

They are all very close. They have a spare key to each of their homes for such cases. For the first time, she feels like something is wrong. Her mind begins to wonder if he is in the hospital, locked up, or worse, dead.

Her cellphone rings again. With each ring, her heart skips a beat. It is Labron.

"Hey, Labron, please tell me he overslept last night." She pauses and listens to the other end of the phone.

He says, "I spoke to the security gate guards. When they checked the systems, they said his gate pass wasn't used to enter the building yesterday."

She shook her head and asks, "Are you sure he didn't go home last night? OK, maybe he got arrested or is in the hospital. I am going to the police station."

She turns her attention to the store manager. "Craig, there is no sign of him. I am going to the police station, maybe he got arrested last night. Just ensure everything runs smoothly. I will be back."

She leaves the establishment and drives to the police station. For the duration of the journey, she is just wondering, *What could Alion have gotten himself into? But then again, he would have called one of us.* She is trying to justify her fears. Since her encounter with the cops, she hates the blue but knows she needs them to help her find her friend.

She walks in through the large glass door and approaches the front desk where a white male police officer is sitting.

He asks, "How can I help you, miss?'

She replies, "Hi, good day. My friend Alion Ross just opened his car dealership and didn't show up for work. He is not answering his cellphone. We checked his apartment and all the places he frequents. No sign of him.

"I know him, and this is out of character. Can you please check your systems and see if he has been arrested or hospitalized or anything else?"

He replies, "Sorry to hear that." He starts typing on his computer keypad. "Please repeat his name."

Majesty answers, "Alion Ross."

"What's his date of birth?"

She replies, "June 15, 1995."

He replies, "Thank you."

He inputs the information into his computer, and in a few seconds, he says, "I am sorry, but there are no arrests or records on that person." He continues, "It has not even been 24 hours yet. He maybe went for a long ride or hooked up with an old girlfriend. Give it some time."

Disappointed with the results, she leaves.

She thinks to herself, *Something is not right. I am going to the hospital to see if he is admitted, but he would have called. I will still go and check.*

CHAPTER 33

Bahamas

Majesty is disappointed with what the police told her, *Wait 24 hours, which is absolutely ridiculous*, she thinks. She can't shake the feeling of worrying. In the pit of her gut, she can feel anxiety overpowering her. Aimlessly, she walks to her car.

She sits in the driver's seat and slouches over the steering wheel. She knows they are a target because of Badaz's murder, and they have a lot of enemies. She is hoping to find the answers to Alion's disappearance. She starts to feel pins and needles in her feet. Suddenly, her cellphone rings. She wiggles her feet to relieve the pain.

Her heart skips a beat, and she reaches for her cellphone. It isn't the news she is hoping for. Before she gets a chance to say hello, she hears screams of horror. Stephany is on the other end of the phone wailing, "They sent his head in a box!"

Majesty is frozen in shock. She is hoping this is one of her regular nightmares. She feels a lump in her throat, and all she can do is cry out, "No!" She immediately ends the call and dials Arthur's number.

He is seemingly waiting for her call, as he picks up on the first ring. "Majesty anything?"

She is muffled, and her crying makes it hard for Arthur to hear her. "Baby, he is dead, Alion is dead. It must be the Faceoff Crew, sending us a very strong message. Baby, they killed him and sent his head to the dealership, the same way we sent Badaz's head back to them."

Arthur goes silent. He, too, is in shock, but he knows the game, and he knew the possible end results. This is one of them. Nonetheless, he can't fight back the tears. Alion was like a brother to him. "Calm down, baby, go back inside and report it to the police. I will meet you at the dealership in an hour."

At this point, she is shaking like a leaf. Her legs wobble as she walks back inside.

She thinks to herself, "These must be the nightmares that I have been getting."

As she enters the police station, shaken up, she explains what she has just learned to the station guard. As she answers all the questions, the tears roll down her cheeks. In a matter of seconds, the officer calls in the address and sends units to the scene. Majesty jumps in her car and drives as fast as she can back to the dealership. She can't help but think about all the fun times they had and how happy he was to open his dealership. The closer she gets to the dealership, the more her anxiety grows. She can hear the police sirens and see the flashing lights.

As she pulls into the parking lot, she sees Arthur, Labron, Stephany, Craig, and all the other employees standing outside, engaging in conversation. They are all devastated.

Majesty leaps out of her car, runs to her husband, and falls into his arms, crying. He shows her the box that is nicely packaged with Alion's head.

The police lights are flashing, and the sirens are so loud. The crime scene is chaotic. The police officers all wear gloves. They cordon off the scene with yellow caution tape, protecting whatever evidence they find. One officer is taking pictures of the scene. Wasting no time in commencing their investigations, they confiscate the box containing Alion's head and start questioning everyone on the scene. Everyone has the same story.

Alion is a good boss; he recently opened his dealership, and no one knows of a reason anyone would want to hurt him.

His unexpected death has left everyone with unanswered questions.

The lead detective approaches them and gives his name as Detective

Alonzo. He has a small notepad on which he occasionally scribbles whatever information he gets. He asks, "You were at the station earlier today, asking about his disappearance? How are you related to Mr. Alion Ross?"

Majesty answers quickly, "Yes, I was there. He is my nephew."

He replies, "Are you aware of anyone who would want him dead? This is a clear message that these people are sending. They could have killed him and disposed of his entire body, but they beheaded him and sent his head here. You guys must be careful."

Arthur reiterates, "Alion was a good man. He wanted to open his business, and someone did this to him as soon as he did it. We don't know anyone who would do such a thing."

Detective Alonzo adds, "A few months ago Badaz, a gang leader from the Faceoff Crew, was murdered similarly. This is no coincidence. Either it is a new trend, or it is some reprisal for his death. Alion may or may not have been connected to Badaz's murder." Majesty and Stephany exchange suspicious glances.

"What kind of vehicle is he driving? At least I can start there."

Craig answers, "He was driving a white Mercedes truck. I was the last person who saw him alive, and he told me he would stop at the corner store and pick up some groceries. Maybe you can check the local stores and see if there is any footage of him."

"Good." The detective continues, "I will get to the bottom of this and let you folks know what I find out." He hands them each a business card. "If anything comes up, please call me. I will try to locate the rest of his body."

Detective Alonzo asks, "Who delivered the package?"

Craig sighs. He peers over at the obviously distraught secretary, "A courier in a khaki uniform. He asked for a signature, and unbeknownst to the receptionist what was in the package, she willingly signed for it."

The detective is very thorough in his work and promises to leave no stone unturned. This could potentially mean trouble for the rest of the crew, but they oblige and comply with his every request.

The detective asks, "Can someone please show me Alion's office?"

Craig takes the detective inside so he can retrieve whatever video footage is there and use it as evidence.

Craig starts to doubt Alion's financial abilities and wonders how a man of his age and means can acquire all this money to open a dealership like this. Maybe he was involved in drugs. Maybe he was involved in something else illegal. It had to be something serious for someone to kill you like that and send your head in a box. He starts to have second thoughts about working at the dealership.

Arthur, Comala, Labron, and Stephany keep exchanging glances. They know exactly the reason Alion died; they just can't tell the cops.

The officer and Craig are in the back office, giving them time to chat. "This is the same way we killed that fucker; how did they know it was us?" asks Stephany.

Majesty scoffs, "Girl, this is a mess. One thing is for sure, they know now."

Labron asks, "So when do we strike back?"

Arthur responds, "They are probably watching us. We can't let this slide; we must fight back!"

They have an unspoken language that only they understand. They all leave in their cars and head in the same direction. Arthur leads the team to a motel about 15 kilometers from the dealership. Majesty approaches the front desk without looking suspicious and checks for vacancies. Arthur is between calls, while Majesty handles the financial aspect of the rooms.

The rest of the team waits for the signal to enter the motel lobby. They don't want to enter and draw attention to themselves as a group.

The team meets in a tiny room. Not one that they are used to, but they have to lie low and keep a low profile. It is extremely important that they stay out of sight for a while.

The room has red carpets and two double beds. No one has plans to sleep, but there is just enough space to meet and calculate their next move.

They all sit on the bed in silence for at least five minutes. No one says anything. They feel shock, fear, anxiety, disgust, regret, and, most importantly, loss. The family of five has now diminished to a family of four.

Is this the beginning of a trend, is it done? Did they get their revenge? Or are they coming back? Either way, they need to be prepared.

Stephany breaks the silence. "He must have confessed to everything when they were killing him. Remember how Badaz told us everything, even his mother's birthday?" Everyone disregards her remark. Arthur signals to Majesty and tells her to call Ms. B.

Majesty and Arthur have a contingency plan for their child. They know the game might get messy, so they prepare for any eventuality. She doesn't hesitate to call.

Before the nanny can properly greet her, she says, "Hello, Ms. B. I want you to listen to me very carefully. Go to my bedroom, look in my closet. In there, you will find three duffle bags. Carry them with you. Open the smaller black bag. You will see a cellphone. I will call you on that phone number moving forward. Please pack enough clothes for you and Demetre. The driver will be downstairs in 20 minutes. He will take you to the airport, and you will meet the private jet where we normally would."

The nanny listens keenly to Majesty's instructions. "You will be taken to the Bahamas when you arrive. A driver there will be waiting. Stay at the hotel, and we will meet you there in a few days. Do not call us. We will call you. Understood?" Majesty asks.

Ms. B answers, "Yes, ma'am."

Majesty ends the call and dials the driver's phone, giving him instructions. She also books the flight and makes a reservation for them to stay at the hotel.

Majesty disconnects the call, takes a deep breath, and gives her husband a nervous glance.

"Are you ready?" Majesty asks. Arthur looks at her and says, "Here we come!"

The somber mood in the motel room is enough to extend beyond the four walls. They have to snap out of it and get down to business. Keeping Demetre safe is their number one priority, and that has already been taken care of. Now, it's time to plan and execute.

Arthur says in a commanding tone, "OK, team, we need to change location in case someone trailed us here. We need to get some weapons. At this point, we need to be hunting them, not them hunting us. It's kill or be killed."

Stephany interjects in a stern voice, "I will go to my crib and grab all my weapons, some black clothes for me and you Majesty, and I will meet you back here."

"No, it's too risky to come back here," says Majesty. "Labron, go with Stephany and collect your weapons too. We cannot afford to be riding alone. That is exactly what they are waiting for."

Arthur says, "Sounds like a good plan. Meet us within an hour at the Comreg Hotel. I will let you know the room number."

Arthur said, "Call us if anything strange happens. Please be careful and watch your surroundings."

Stephany grabs her keys, and as a distraction, she and Labron exit the property arm in arm, pretending to be husband and wife.

They take Labron's truck and head toward Stephany's house first.

On the way, they both freely express themselves. Labron says, "Yow, Steph, I can't believe those motherfuckers killed Alion."

Stephany replies in a sad voice, "You're right, Labron. He was like a brother to me. To us, he was family. It hurts because he suffered before he died. It is evident in his face. They tortured him."

Labron is watching his rearview mirror to ensure no one is following. He is paranoid and takes several roads just to be safe.

He turns into Stephany's apartment complex. The security recognizes them and proceeds to open the gate.

They examine their surroundings before exiting the truck. They have to be extra careful. Once the environs seem clear, they enter her apartment. Labron stands guard at the door while she retrieves what she needs.

At this junction, they need to be armed and prepared. She changes into some tennis shoes and puts on her bulletproof vest and all-black outfit.

She equips herself with a bag of money, a small handgun, a submachine gun, an AK-47, a Uzi, a Desert Eagle, silencers, and ammunition. She grabs two bulletproof vests for Majesty and Arthur, places everything in a duffle bag, and takes a black sweatsuit for Majesty to change into.

It is time to go to Labron's home. They do their due diligence before getting into the truck. They continue to check their surroundings intermittently.

When they get to his apartment, it is less tedious as they don't have to wait for security to let them in. They move as briskly as they can, checking at short intervals to ensure they are not being followed. He opens his door, and they hurriedly go inside and secure the lock.

He grabs all the weapons he can. He has to prepare for whatever is coming.

Like Stephany, he arms himself before leaving the house. He changes, puts on his bulletproof vest and a black outfit, and brings a black outfit for Arthur. He grabs some walkie-talkies and tasers. They are sure to conceal the bags they packed in the event they are pulled over by the cops.

Stephany dials Majesty's number. Everyone is on edge. Majesty answers on the first ring. She sounds timid. "Steph, are you guys OK?" she asks.

"Yes, sis, we are OK. We got the money and all the weapons. Do you want us to come to The Comreg Hotel Spa now?"

Majesty responds, "Yes, the room number is 3709."

They quickly end the call.

Majesty and Arthur are already at the ComReg Hotel, armed and ready to fight. The room is much nicer than the motel they were congregating in earlier. Despite the current happenings, Majesty is still a concerned wife.

"Baby, you know you cannot be putting so much pressure on your heart, the doctor warned us, remember? Do you want to meet up with Ms. B. and Demetre in the Bahamas? I will take care of this. This game is nasty, and I don't want the worst-case scenario where Demetre ends up as an orphan," says Majesty.

Arthur rebuts, "Are you kidding me, Majesty? I am not leaving you here, and we will not go down. At the end of the fight, we will be going home to our son. Labron and Stephany will be going home to their families. We must kill all those motherfuckers tonight."

Arthur continues, "Honey, remember when we were killing Badaz? He squealed like a pussy, he told us everything we asked him. That shitbag even told his mother's birthday and said his ABCs. He is a bitch; he had no choice."

She chuckles slightly. "Alion was our family. We must fight for him. It is time to end this and kill every one of them."

She smirks. She loves it when he calls her honey; it turns her on. They have just enough time to make love and release their sadness and frustration before the rest of the team gets there.

CHAPTER 34

Look Yah!

rthur and Majesty are exhausted from the passionate lovemaking and the day's events. But they have no time to sleep. Labron and Stephany are in the lobby heading up. When they get to the hotel room, they have the bags with the money and weapons. Arthur says, "OK listen up, they killed Alion. If we don't stop these fuckers, they will keep on coming at us."

"Badaz caused his own death. He came to us posing threats and tried to extort our operations. We had no choice. He killed innocent people, so we had to retaliate." He continues, "Tonight, we strike back, and this time, we kill everyone in that washed-up Faceoff Crew."

Majesty says, "Stephany, your informer friend Kirk that hangs out over there, call him and see if you can get any information on what is going on over there."

Stephany obliges and dials her childhood friend's number.

Kirk's phone keeps ringing and ringing, no answer. She rings it until it goes to voicemail.

"Coward," Labron grumbles under his breath.

Majesty chimes in, "Forget him. We need to eat and get some rest. We need all the energy we can for tomorrow, plus, at least if we die, we die with a belly full."

This makes everyone laugh. It feels good to express an emotion other than crying.

She continues, "So here is the plan. We will leave at 3 a.m. It is now 9:45 p.m. Stephany, you, and Labron will go in first and shoot everyone. Leave no stone unturned. Arthur and I will cover you guys. We will be behind to finish up."

Arthur has created a plan on a sheet of paper; he is showing Labron what angle to attack from based on the setup of the club. Meanwhile, Majesty is busy ordering food.

Majesty orders chicken, steak, lobster, shrimp, corn, vegetables, mashed potato, and two bottles of wine and a red rose. In about an hour, there is a knock on the door. Everyone stops what they are doing and draws their gun.

"Room service," a male voice on the other side of the door says. Everyone stops what they are doing and takes their guns out. They have to play it safe; it could be anyone. After all, they are targets.

Majesty walks to the door and holds a gun behind her. Arthur stands to her right with his gun ready, while Labron stands behind the door.

She peeps through the hole in the door and notices it is a man of Mexican descent dressed in a black and white uniform with a white glove. He stands at the door with a cart loaded with food and the wine they ordered. Majesty tells everyone to stand down and open the door.

She opens the door for him. "Good evening, madam. Your order is ready."

He pushes the cart inside the room and places the food on the counter. He is very polite and professional. He gives her the red rose she requested.

She says, "Thank you." She tips him handsomely, and he leaves the room a happy man. The meal looks so appetizing. The aroma is tempting, yet no one has an appetite. They all miss Alion, and the thought of not having him around makes them sad.

They eat bits and pieces while they cross their t's and dot their I's to ensure they are successful with their plans.

The time is moving quickly. They don't realize it is winding down. After dinner and planning it is 1:45 a.m. There isn't enough time to rest; it is do or die. Labron pushes the food cart outside the room, and they start to equip themselves with the necessary protective gear. They dress in bulletproof vests, packing the guns and screwing the silencers on the guns. They don't want to create a "scene." Once they are ready, everyone is given a walkie-talkie so they can communicate their every move.

Stephany and Labron take a quick break after getting ready. They lie on the bed in silence, staring at the ceiling. Arthur is pacing back and forth and keeps looking at his watch. Majesty, on the other hand, is not losing any sleep. She naps for 30 minutes. She remembers her parents.

At approximately 2:30 p.m., Arthur wakes her up and says, "It's time to go!" Stephany and Labron pack one set of weapons in Labron's truck and another set with the bags of money in Arthur's Benz truck. Majesty puts the rose in her pocket. They have to be discreet in their operations, lest anyone find out.

Arthur drives his truck, and Labron follows behind. The roads are clear. Only a few partygoers and drunken drivers can be seen speeding recklessly. They don't want to cause any unwanted attention to themselves, so they follow the speed limit and take their time.

They exit the highway and make a stop at an intersection, waiting for the traffic lights to change. Arthur is in the lead, with Majesty in the front passenger seat. Suddenly a black Dodge drives up beside Arthur. He seemingly attempts to roll his windows down.

Arthur and Majesty are ready to pop off. They both have their handguns in their laps, and with just the touch of the trigger, Majesty is ready to fight. He can see Labron in his rearview mirror, and notices he, too is uneasy. Luckily, the light changes to green, and the car speeds off. Arthur takes a deep breath.

Labron continues to trail Arthur's vehicle.

When they arrive at the Asylum Club headquarters, it is exactly 3 a.m. Six men are celebrating outside. It is a quiet night. There isn't much of a crowd.

They park and wait eagerly for the right time to go inside. They have to be strategic. It is four of them, and God knows how many are inside.

Majesty begins to give orders via the walkie-talkies.

"There are six men at the front, Stephany. Use your charm. You walk up to them and distract them. Labron, use that as the opportunity to start shooting them. By the time you pop off, they will try to reach for their guns, so Steph, as soon as Labron starts shooting, you start too. Arthur and I will take care of the ones you can't handle. We are at a vantage point."

"Roger that," Stephany replies.

She looks at Labron and asks, "Are you ready?"

He replies, "As ready as I'll ever be."

She jumps out of the truck and walks up to the men standing at the door. All of them look in her direction, coming closer to them. One of the men asks, "Hey beautiful, are you lost? The club is closed tonight, or are you coming to see me, honey?"

Stephany continues walking. She is playing the same trick she did on Badaz. "Closed? So soon? I really need a drink, maybe some Sex on the Beach!" The men flirt and laugh. Stephany whispers in the tall fellow's ears. "Hey, cutie, how is your night?"

He doesn't get a chance to answer. She tases him while Labron sneaks up and starts to shoot. Stephany pops off and shoots two of the men as they struggle to retrieve their weapons. The man who was tased isn't dead; he is reaching for his firearm, Majesty notices from a distance. She aims and shoots him in his head.

They've cleaned up the outside; now on to the big dogs.

Labron and Stephany step over the bodies and proceed to enter the club as quietly as they can. Through their devices, they inform Majesty and Arthur that they are inside.

She reloads the gun as she walks briskly. Labron is behind, checking for unwanted guests. The dance floor is empty, but they can hear chatter in the distance. Possibly coming from the back office.

As they approached the back office, there is a VIP area. Two guys are chilling and having a drink. Labron catches them off guard and shoots one in the head while Stephany shoots the other in his chest. There is blood everywhere; a man sitting in the room adjacent to them hears one of the men groan and raises an alarm.

Binns comes out of the room and fires a shot, hitting Stephany in the shoulder; she makes a loud sound. This alerts Adisha and his cronies, who are in the back office. Adisha knows they are under attack.

Labron shoots after Binns twice and tries to aid Stephany, but the Faceoff crew comes out strong and starts spraying bullets. They both go for cover behind a sofa in the lounge. The men are shooting and withholding nothing.

Stephany is hurt, but she is fighting back. They both start shooting back, hitting a few of the Jungles members and killing them. They need backup, and they need a better place to hide.

Labron says, "Cover me while I run to that side because we need to attack from a different angle."

As he runs off to the safe spot, he runs straight into Binns. Stephany shouts, "Labron, look out!" It is too late; she is too late. Binns shoots him in the head, and he falls to the floor.

Stephany is devastated. Even though she is hurt, she finds the strength to shoot. She sprays bullets everywhere. One of the bullets lodges in Binns' chest, and he falls to the floor beside Labron. She runs to see if Binns is dead; she shoots him in the head three times to ensure he doesn't survive. She keeps calling for backup on the walkie-talkie while reloading her clip. *This is a fucking massacre*, she thinks.

Labron is dead.

CHAPTER 35
Another One!

There is blood everywhere. Dead bodies are everywhere. Time stands still in the chaotic situation for Stephany. When she sees Labron's lifeless body lying on the floor, she screams his name. "Labron, noooo!" She places her head on his chest, hoping for a heartbeat. Nothing. There is none.

Stephany is so caught up in the moment that she doesn't notice a man behind her aiming his gun to shoot. Her childhood friend Kirk sees what is happening. He tries to fire his gun sparingly as he doesn't want to hurt Stephany, nor does he want to give away his cover. But when he sees that Stephany is about to get shot, he fires his gun, killing one of his own crew members.

Adisha is just in time to see this. He feels betrayed. In a matter of seconds, he shouts, "TRAITOR!" and opens fire, killing Kirk on the spot, and runs for cover.

Majesty and Arthur come in and start firing shots, taking out all the men in sight.

Majesty shakes her head, and she sees another one of her friend's lifeless bodies in a pool of blood. She feels an unimaginable rage come over her, and she starts to scream and spray bullets, this time using two guns at once.

Stephany is losing her strength; she is hiding behind a column close to Labron's body and crying. With her husband acting as her shield, Majesty goes to Stephany and says, "Let's go, he is dead!"

Arthur shakes his head when he sees Labron, and quickly moves past him, scrutinizing the room, looking for anything that moves. They hurry to get cover, giving Stephany the opportunity to charge her gun for the next victim.

Majesty takes the lead. She sees three men on the staircase with guns aiming at them. She shoots them so fast the shots penetrate their heads, necks, and chests. They all come rolling down the stairs.

She steps over the bodies piled up on the floor, heading upstairs to the upper deck of the club. Arthur and Stephany are right behind her. As she reaches the top flight of the staircase, she notices a private room on her right. The door is ajar, and she pushes it open enough to scan the room looking for the next asshole. It is empty.

Out of nowhere, Adisha appears, grabs Stephany from behind, and points his gun to her head. He doesn't even negotiate but fires the gun and blows her brains out right in front of Majesty.

Poor Majesty's heart sinks. She takes a deep breath. It isn't over; she still has to fight for her life and her husband's life. She doesn't have time to be sad.

She looks down on Stephany in disbelief. She holds her composure and pulls the trigger four times. Click-click-click-click. There is no fucking bullet left in her gun.

That gives Adisha a chance to run for cover.

Arthur shoots at him, but he misses. He takes refuge behind a wall. In a loud voice, Adisha shouts, "You murdered my best friend and cut his head off, well, I hope you enjoyed the package that I sent you. That fucker was so brave, we tortured him, and he didn't say a word. You trained your dogs well. Too bad you couldn't save them. He took it like a man. He didn't say a word. I lift my hat off to him. He took it like a soldier."

This angers Arthur, but he rebuts and laughs, "On the contrary, Badaz sang like a fucking bird, that asshole couldn't hold it, when we were pulling his nails out one by one, he told us everything, he cried like a bitch, he even told even what he had for dinner, he told us his mother's birthday."

That makes Adisha so mad he fires a couple of rounds at them and says, "I am going to kill both of you."

Majesty reloads and is ready again. They both open fire at Adisha. They both miss.

Adisha is still so angered by the way Arthur tried to humiliate Badaz.

He runs over to Majesty, punches her in the face, and kicks her to the ground. She gets up, kicks him in the groin area, and punches him in the face with all her might.

Arthur is aiming at him but doesn't want to hit Majesty.

Adisha grabs Majesty's throat and tries to squeeze her life out. Majesty is wrestling with him. She tells herself she will not die without trying.

Try as Arthur may, he can't get a clear shot. With one hand having Majesty in a chokehold, Adisha uses his other hand to aim at Arthur. He hits the target on his first shot.

Arthur is shot in the side of his neck. She sees her husband collapse to the floor.

Majesty closes her eyes so tight, hoping when she reopens them, it will turn out to be a dream. Unfortunately, it isn't.

She finds the strength she needs. "I am going to fucking kill you."

He replies, "Bitch, did you think you were going to get away with my best friend's murder? I am going to kill you the way all your friends died, one by one, you whore."

As he continues to strangle her, he slaps her in frustration and throws her to the floor.

She tries to regain her strength, but he kicks her in the stomach, causing her to crouch in pain.

Each time she tries to get up, he throws another blow, causing her to fall again. It is over for her, she thinks.

Majesty is now only one of the bodies on the ground.

Splash

A cold liquid splashes against her face, causing her to gasp for air. She wakes up, feeling relief, thinking it is all a dream. She tells herself, "It is just another one of those dreadful nightmares."

Except this time, it isn't. It is real. Alion, Labron, Stephany, and Arthur are all dead, and she is tied up in the middle of the club, surrounded by dead bodies. Hands and feet bound. It feels all too familiar.

Adisha punches her in the face and breaks her nose. The pain is excruciating, and blood is running down her face.

He says in an intimidating voice, "I am going to make you suffer."

Majesty sits in agony, reminiscing on every memory she ever had, from the day she was born to growing up and meeting her husband. She slowly gathers strength.

She rocks slowly from side to side in pain as though she were soothing the pain. He continues to throw blows.

Adisha is now over the theatrics and decides it is time to start torturing her. While searching for the pliers, he speaks in an evil tone.

"This is your last morning; I am going to finish you."

She quietly rocks her right hand from side to side, trying to break loose from the poorly tied bondage. Thinking about Demetre, she tries again and again. BINGO! She breaks free. She quickly unties the rope, binding her leg, and slowly reaches into her pocket for the taser. She places her hand back in the position as if she is still restrained.

She is so calculated.

He turns around and aims to give her another blow, but he is too late. She removes her taser and points it in his chest, and she gives him the shock of his life. He falls to the ground, unconscious.

She has no mercy on him. He killed her husband and her close friends. He needs to be dead. Not presumed dead, but dead.

She runs to the closest available loaded gun, stands over him, and thinks of all the pain he caused her, including almost leaving her son parentless.

She says, "Die bitch," and fires two rounds, not caring where they lodge. She spits a mouth full of blood in his face. She quickly runs over to where Arthur is, crying, "Arthur, please wake up." She gives him mouth-to-mouth resuscitation and practices chest compression, hoping to get a pulse. She applies pressure to his wound to stop the bleeding. She repeats the process, and finally, she gets a faint pulse. She says, "Thank you, God!"

He barely opens his eyes. He is conscious. It's a good thing she took classes with Miss Mary all those years. She had strength, that is for sure. That is all she needs to get him to the nearest emergency room.

She says, "Let's get out of here, baby."

She helps him up, gently walks with him down the stairs, and puts him in his Benz truck.

She goes back to check on Stephany and Labron, just to be sure she isn't leaving anyone behind. She has to double-check that they are indeed dead.

Majesty isn't about to leave empty-handed; she searches the offices and takes all three duffle bags of money, plus jewelry and any valuables she can find.

She packs them in the truck, but she isn't finished. She has to clean up the mess, leaving little or no evidence pointing towards them.

She goes back in with a bottle of gasoline and a match. She sprinkles the bodies with gasoline the same way Miss Mary taught her; it reminds her of when she burned down Bob's house. It is hard for her, as her friends are inside, but she has to do what she has to do. Majesty takes the red rose from her pocket and throws it on Adisha's body. The same way she did to Bob's body.

She exits the building and strikes the match. She sees her deepest fears unfold through that tiny flame, but they end this morning. She throws the match back and runs as fast as she can toward her truck. The Asylum Night Club is engulfed in flames. She has no time to celebrate. She looks through her rearview mirror and sees the fire from a distance. She drives to a lonely road; she quickly takes off her and Arthur's bullet-proof vests.

She cleans up as much blood as she can from their hands and faces, removing evidence to the best of her ability; after all, she doesn't want to go to prison. After cleaning the evidence, she talks to her husband to keep him awake; she doesn't want the hospital to ask any questions.

She continues on the route to the hospital. She stops on a bridge and throws the vests and any extra bloody clothes into the water. It's a good thing they are wearing black.

CHAPTER 36

Despair

O n her way to the hospital, she passes police cars and fire
trucks racing in the opposite direction, heading to Asylum
Night Club. She drives like lightning. When she arrives at
the hospital, she turns her hazard lights on and honks her horn. Three
paramedics come out to help them. They waste no time putting Arthur
on a stretcher and wheel him to the emergency room.

While they are running with him, another paramedic questions her.
She is in excruciating pain. "Madam, what happened?"

She replies tearfully, "Someone tried to rob me and my husband. My
husband put up a fight, but they shot him in his neck and beat me
badly. I need some medical attention too."

The paramedic asks, "What is your husband's name, and how old
is he?"

She replies, "Arthur Bitting, and he is thirty-three years old. He was
a patient here before. You guys treated him for a heart attack."

The paramedic quickly gets her a wheelchair so she can sit and rolls
her into the emergency lobby.

The triage nurse takes her vitals and carefully dresses her wounds.
She is trying to make conversation with her, but everything is a blur.
Majesty is lost in her own world. She thinks to herself, *I can't believe*

everyone is dead, Stephany, Labron, and Alion, oh my God, what do I do now, I can't believe this. Tears flow down her cheeks.

The nurse says, "Ms. Bitting, everything will be just fine, I will check on your husband for you when I am done dressing your wounds and broken nose. I highly suggest that when you get discharged, you make a police report."

The thought of the police getting involved before they have a chance to leave town gives her the extra energy she needs. She is not trying to have law enforcement investigate them.

She replies, "Thank you, I will. I'm fine now. Can you please check on my husband?"

As soon as the nurse leaves the room, she dials the nanny's number.

She answers, "Hello, Ms. Bitting. Is everything OK?"

Majesty replies, "Everything is just fine. I will see you in a few days. I am just taking care of some unfinished business."

Ms. B replies, "Demetre is sleeping. Do you want me to wake him?"

Majesty says, "No, I'm in the middle of something. I will spend some quality time with him when we arrive. See you soon." She hangs up the phone.

Majesty thinks to herself, *Those Faceoff Crew fools would not stop. They would have killed all of us if we hadn't put a stop to them.* Majesty feels satisfied she burned that operation down.

The nurse asks her if she is on any medication. She leaves the room, returns in 15 minutes, and hands her two pills for her pain and a cup of water.

"Take these, and they will ease the pain. I will put you in a temporary room for the doctor to see you."

"How is my husband? How is he doing?" she asks.

"I don't know. I will let you know as soon as I hear something," says the nurse. The nurse leads her to a room with a curtain and says, "Please wait for the doctor."

Majesty sits on the hospital bed. She prays in a quiet voice and begs the Lord to have mercy. "Lord, please spare my husband's life." Shortly, the doctor knocks and walks into her room.

"Hi, Ms. Bitting. I am Dr. Buckley. How are you feeling? I heard what happened to you and your husband. He will be fine. We just operated on him, and he is resting. All I can say is, he is a very lucky man."

She says, "Thank God he is doing OK."

Majesty wants to leave so badly. With the pills, the nurse gave her, she feels no pain. She needs to get Arthur before the police get there.

She replies, "Thank you so much. Can I see him now?"

Dr. Buckley says again, "Yes, after the nurse finishes cleaning up your wounds, I will discharge you."

The nurse comes in with more gauze, and Band-Aids.

Majesty thanks her.

The nurse leaves, returns in a few minutes, and hands her the discharge papers. She leads her to the hallway and up an elevator. They enter a room, and she marches in behind her. Arthur is lying on the bed, sleeping, with a bandage on his neck.

She rushes over to the bed and kisses him.

The nurse says, "I will leave you now. You stay by his side until he wakes up."

She replies quickly, "I want him to get as much rest as he can."

As soon as the nurse leaves the room, she tries to wake him up. She gently shakes him.

She whispers, "Arthur, Arthur, Arthur, wake up, baby, we have to go now, please wake up!"

He slightly opens his eyes. Everything is blurry; he is still under anesthesia.

He recognizes Majesty. He says softly in a weak voice, "Honey, where am I?"

She replies, "Baby, you're in the hospital. Remember that asshole shot you. He killed everyone, we must get out of here, right now."

He feels a shooting pain in his neck.

He says, "Oh, oh shit! I thought I was dreaming. Where is he now? Are you sure the others are dead?"

She replies, "Yes, I checked everyone. They are all gone, babe." Tears run down her cheeks. "I killed that son of a bitch, and I went back in Badaz's office. He had three bags of money, cocaine, and jewelry. I took everything. I burnt that bitch down! I will explain the details later, honey. We must leave now!"

He now understands the urgency. He asks, "Did you say anything to the doctors?"

She replies, "Absolutely not. I told them some men tried to rob us, and they shot you and beat me up."

He replies, "You are so smart."

She says, "I am going to call them in now. Pretend you are OK and let them discharge you. The doctor says you are free to go once you wake up."

He says, "You got it, let's do it."

She presses the help button, and a nurse comes in immediately. She is astonished to see Arthur up so fast.

She says, "Mr. Bitting, how are you doing?"

He replies with a smile and a firm voice, "Couldn't be better. I feel like a new man." They all laugh.

The nurse replies, "Great to know. Let me call the doctor in for you."

A few minutes later, the doctor comes in.

He says, "Hello again, how are you doing, Mr. Bitting? I almost lost you there. Now, you will feel pain occasionally, but continue to take the prescribed drugs, and they will help with the pain. I want you to follow up with your primary care doctor. The most difficult part of your surgery is keeping your heart rate stable; other than that it went great. I want to keep you in overnight for observation."

Arthur rebuts quickly, "No, I am feeling great. Can you discharge me? I want to go to the police station with my wife and get those hoodlums off the street."

The doctor says, "OK, if you feel that way, I can only advise you. Remember you had heart surgery this year, and you are still healing, but I cannot hold you against your will, so I will have a nurse process your discharge and come with your prescription. All the best, Mr. Bitting."

He replies, "Thank you, Doc."

The doctor nods, smiles, and exits the room.

Not long after, a nurse enters the room and starts to remove all the cords attached to him as well as the IV port. He cuts Arthur's registration band off and hands him a discharge paper with his prescription.

The nurse says, "You will feel cramps from time to time. Just keep taking your medication, and it will gradually disappear. No swimming or long showers, just stay out of water for a little while. Please be safe out there."

Majesty replies, "Thanks a lot." The nurse leaves the room.

Majesty quickly helps him out of bed and assists him in putting on his clothes and shoes. He is in so much pain but has to pretend he is fine.

She gives Arthur support to get up, and they both sneak slowly out of the hospital. She tells him to sit on the hospital bench while she pulls up the truck.

He says, "Baby, Alion, Stephany, and Labron are all gone. Damn, I can't believe it's just me and you right now. What do we do now?"

She pauses. "Baby, I don't have all the answers right now. I just want to see my son."

He gently rubs her leg. "Me too, me too."

She continues, "One thing is for sure, and two things are for certain, I don't want to live like this anymore. Arthur, we just lost all of our close friends, Alion, Labron, and Stephany." Distraught, she says, "We have enough money to live comfortably for the rest of our lives. Let us sell out every single business and move to another state."

Arthur agrees. He knows it is time to hang up his hat.

She remembers the day he had a heart attack and the prayer she prayed silently. She remembers the promise she made to God and that she broke it. Is it karma?

CHAPTER 37
Redemption

No human being is so bad, as to be beyond redemption.
-Mahatma Gandhi

As a child, it was mandatory for Majesty to attend Sunday school with her grandmother after the passing of her parents. She eventually stopped going. The last thing her mother did before she died was pray for her.

Majesty, however, knew the principles of the Bible and believed in God.

As a child, she was raised to "Do right, act right and say right!" This followed her through her teenage years, but somewhere along the line, things changed.

As she grew older, she remained steadfast in her belief that God can save you from any stressful situation and sometimes even save you from yourself.

Prayer changes things, she thought. When she was stranded on the highway years ago, she prayed that God would send honest people to help, and He did.

When she was in the house with Alion, the rest of her friends, and the police came, she prayed, asking God to get her out of the situation.

At the time, it seemed as if God had failed her, as she was incarcerated for a period. Again, she prayed silently, asking God to help her. She was once again rescued as the charges were dropped.

After getting married to the love of her life, everything was bliss. But then, Arthur had a heart attack.

Majesty was exasperated, but for a split second, her faith increased. In the same hospital waiting room, she made a promise to God to do right if her husband was healed.

God indeed answers prayers. Arthur was subsequently released from the hospital.

Majesty quickly forgot her promise and returned to a life of sin and illegal activities.

Her life took a turn for the worst, and everyone was now dead! Alion, Stephany, and Labron were all dead. And her parents.

Quickly, she remembered a powerful scripture, "The Lord disciplines those He loves, and He punishes each one He accepts as His child"(Hebrews 12:6).

"I am His child!" Majesty realized she was indeed His child.

After losing her friends and coming face to face with death on so many different occasions, plus almost losing her husband, Majesty decided she needed to keep true to her promise to God.

* * *

The couple decided to sell their assets and moved to Miami. It was a refreshing feeling, and they were now ready to start fresh with their son.

Through all their ordeals, they experienced some eventsthat would set the pace for their future.

In honor of Stephany, they set up a foundation named "Stephany's Bail Out." This foundation was geared toward assisting inmates who had no family to bail them out. There were conditions to their bail; however, they had to be rehabilitated and stay out of trouble.

They opened a ministry in honor of Winnie, Dehon, Alion, and Labron. They offered hot meals to homeless people and mentored young adults who felt unmotivated. They didn't want anyone else to end up on the path they had trod.

Life is now close to perfect. Demetre is healthy and growing, soon to be a big brother to twins.

Majesty and Arthur are giving back to their community!

What could possibly go wrong?

Eighty-eight-year-old Majesty has finished her story.

About the Author

Comala Remogene is from Waterford Portmore, Jamaica. She migrated to the United States, moving to Pembroke Pines, Florida. God is the center of her life. She enjoys spending time at the beach, reading, watching a good movie, listening to every genre of music, and interacting with her readers.

You can email her at:
Callhermajesty1@gmail.com